4.8
1

Princess Ashley

Princess Ashley

RICHARD PECK

DELACORTE PRESS/NEW YORK

Published by
Delacorte Press
1 Dag Hammarskjold Plaza
New York, New York 10017

Manufactured in the United States of America
First printing

Library of Congress Cataloging in Publication Data

Peck, Richard [date of birth]
    Princess Ashley.

    Summary: In her new high school, where her mother has taken
a job as counselor, Chelsea experiences joys and sorrows as she
makes choices about new friends and learns they are not always
what they seem.
    [1. High schools—Fiction. 2. Schools—Fiction. 3. Friend-
ship—Fiction. 4. Moving, Household—Fiction] I. Title.
PZ7.P338Pr 1987   [Fic]   86-29064
ISBN 0-385-29561-8

With thanks for their help to
Courtney Hughes
and
Ann and Aaron Biggers

Sophomore Year

Chapter One

Mom was just as tense as I was. In the car she'd been playing the same tape for two days, the golden oldy hits of, I think, 1970—Led Zeppelin, the Stones, B. B. King. I pretended not to listen, but had to remember not to tap my foot. Mom left sweat marks on the steering wheel.

We were on a thousand-mile trip in the Dodge, pulling a U-Haul trailer. And so it was two years ago, just about now. August before tenth grade in a new school, and a new town.

Was it the Michael Jackson year or the Prince year? No, it was the Madonna year, because I was wearing Madonna earrings—with a sleeveless sweatshirt over cutoff jeans. I'd already won the ear-piercing battle with Mom. But she'd allowed only one puncture per lobe, another grudge I was holding against her.

I was a blonde, but not a fun-in-the-sun blonde. Be-

3

fore I made any changes with my hair, I was waiting to see what they did at this new school. I wasn't even into regular shampooing.

And I thought I was a mile too tall and getting taller on this trip. I thought my head would break through the roof of the Dodge and my knees would grow into the glove compartment.

I was a young fifteen, and so I was crowded way over against the door as far from my mom as I could get. We were heading for this new high school in this new place, and so I sat there slumped, applying mental brakes. I was so desperate I was getting nostalgic for ninth grade.

That was the year I pretty much hated everything: my mother, my looks, even my name: Chelsea Olinger. I hated that name. Chelsea? It wasn't even a name. Nobody had it. It was a place in England Mom had picked up from a book. Mom again.

When I was in grade school, I thought she was great. She was this big, pretty person who was always busy, but always there. Her clothes were nice, and I liked playing in her jewelry box. She doesn't have that much jewelry, but I thought it was just right because she'd picked it. I'd stick all her pins and things on my T-shirt and *be* her.

We got along fine till I was fourteen. Around then I began to think she was coming into my room, going through my stuff. She didn't do that, and I really knew it. But I kept listening to the part of me that believed it. At fourteen you can believe anything you want. I thought I wanted her out of my way. I thought she was standing between me and growing up.

Being in the car for two days straight with her wasn't my favorite thing either. I could have waited to ride with Dad and Lucy. Dad was a day behind us in his truck with our furniture. The load included the canopied bed I'd campaigned for in seventh grade. The corniness of a canopied bed was just beginning to occur to me.

I could have waited and squeezed in with Dad and big overweight Lucy, but in some weird way I didn't want to let Mom out of my sight. I didn't want her around, and I didn't like her the way she was, but I was afraid she was going to change. Something like that.

Just in case there might be something scenic to see, I kept my head down and my eyes on my lap. The car wheels set up a rhythm on the Interstate, even making words. I listened, and the whining tires seemed to be saying: *Friends, friends, friends.*

I knew what that meant. Who was I going to know in this new place, especially in my situation? Who was going to know me? I'd had a few friends in junior high, but that had been different. We'd promised to keep in touch forever. Now I was wondering if I'd remembered to bring their addresses.

When we were getting close, Mom pulled off for gas and took her carryall into the rest room. She came out wearing a fresh blouse and a skirt instead of shorts. So she was edgy, too, gearing up.

As she walked back over the frying-pan pavement, I watched her under hooded lids, fifteenishly. Tall though I am, she's taller, so I guessed I had her to blame for that too. She's probably young-looking for her age and kind of loose-limbed when she moves. You could almost see in her the young girl she'd been, if you were looking. Now she was walking carefully across the parking lot with a neatness that made me nervous.

The sun caught the reddish lights in her hair. They say redheads have tempers, but I could usually handle her. I figured if I got the last word, I was winning. I was also pretty sure we didn't look anything alike apart from the tallness. For one thing, she had a figure. She put her head back to feel the sun on her face. She tans better than I do.

When we got back on the highway, the air-conditioning in the Dodge died. She rolled down her window and propped her elbow outside, trying to keep cool under one arm. I'd started shaving under my arms, recently, and they itched where I'd nicked myself. I knew we were in for it when she reached over and popped the tape out.

"Let's talk a little sense while there's still time."

I groaned.

"We're starting over, so why not do it right?" She used her calmest, most reasonable voice, which I hated.

"It's what I've decided, so forget trying to change my mind," I said, staring out the window. Since I'd looked last, the landscape had gotten big and western with nothing to look at.

"It's childish, you know. And dishonest. And it won't work."

"It'll work," I said, "if you don't spoil it, which you probably will."

Mom ran her fingers through her hair, and it fell back in place because it always does. "Look, it's going

6

to be a much bigger town than you're used to, and Crestwood's a big high school. Everything's going to look enormous to you, but only at first. What you think you want won't work. We can't be . . . anonymous. People are going to find out you're my daughter. People are going to know what I do for a living. You'll just feel silly when they find out. You've blown this thing completely out of proportion. You're older now. You want to be older. Act older."

"Just make sure you're not the one to tell anybody," I said, trying to make it a threat.

But her eyes were on the road, and now she was only half talking to me. "It's not even the job I want. It's the job I could get. I just hope it'll lead to something better."

Spare me your career ambitions, I said, but not out loud. "Just give me a break, okay?"

"I'm trying to give you one now," she said, but that went right over my head. "Don't manufacture problems. You'll have enough real ones."

"Such as?"

"There'll be a lot of kids in this school from well-to-do families. It's that kind of area. They won't all be wealthy, but the wealthy ones are always noticeable. I'll be making a better salary, but not that much better."

"I'm not always begging for things," I muttered.

"I know that," she said. "The problem isn't what rich kids have. It's what rich kids are."

She glanced across at me, and I suspected she was smiling her let's-lighten-up smile. She can see a lot in a glance. And so she saw the big blue glass sets of my crazy earrings, the yawning mouth of my sweatshirt, my mile-long legs disappearing down into off-brand sneakers.

"Just don't spoil high school for me."

"Only you can do that," she said, but it went right over my head too. I was fifteen.

Chapter Two

In tenth grade we said *awesome* a lot. So I suppose it was awesome that the first person I met was Craig Kettering. He was about to be as famous as a sophomore can get, and he glittered when he walked. He was our own Rob Lowe with a little of Bruce Springsteen around the arms. He was also just a kid like the rest of us, but nobody ever noticed that.

Did I have a crush on him? Maybe for a minute, before I pulled myself together. Maybe I had a little fantasy, but he was like somebody up on a stage with the spotlight full on him. And I was down there in the dark, looking up.

I met Craig because of Dad. He was in business before Mom was. Her career came first, which didn't seem right to me. But after she got her job, Dad came out and found his. He deals in hunting dogs. It's not a job for an ambitious man, as he always says, but he's good at it. He trains them, doctors them a little, boards them, sells them to hunters and would-be hunters.

I've grown up around yapping packs of dogs with the smell of the kennel in my nose. I know a little about them myself. There are dogs that point game and dogs that only retrieve. We deal with pointers. The pay's not that great, but a house was part of the deal. The business is Pforzheimer's Kennels, and the last of the Pforzheimers is an old man living in Florida. The place is on the grounds of a big spread, part ranch, part estate. The main house is empty, and the acreage runs back up into the foothills. In the southwest you can get good hunting country that near town.

Dad takes the dogs out to train them. He has to get them easy with a gun. They learn the basics: how to flush game and not to run deer. When I was still in grade school, he tried to make a hunter out of me. But when the dog pointed and the game rose, I always got teary.

"You'll never hunt," he said. "You pity the bird." But he's a little soft on the bird, too, and only hunts to train the dogs.

We live at the rear of the property up the end of a dusty lane that runs down to Artesia Avenue and the paved streets of town. It's the kennelman's old house, just a wing of the kennels with two small bedrooms up under the eaves, and a bathroom. The dog run is right out our windows. Downstairs is mainly one room, long and low with Spanishy beams and an oversized fireplace. The kitchen's at one end behind a round pine table that was already there. That part had linoleum, but Mom scraped it up. The floors are all oak, polished by time and traffic and puppy paws.

In the first days before she started her job, she made the place livable. We didn't have much furniture, and there wasn't enough headroom for the canopy of my bed. Mom set up their wedding picture next to the bed in their room, which meant we were home here. It was just a snapshot, blown up. Mom and Dad are standing by a boat-shaped car, grinning into the sun. Her dress is above her knees, and there are hollows in his cheeks that aren't there now. He has both his arms around her, a bear hug. I never liked that picture.

Mom sewed a pair of Indian blankets together for a throw to go over the sofa and found a couple of stone jars to rig up as lamps. She made curtains out of unbleached muslin. She sort of made something out of nothing.

"You should have been one of those interior decorators," Dad told her.

How true, I thought. What a good idea.

They hooked up their ancient sound system, which they still call the "hi-fi," and one time I came downstairs and they were dancing. I admit, it's a perfect floor, but parents? Dancing? Dad weighs in at about two hundred and twenty pounds. Also he limps. He has a bad knee—gimpy. But they were dancing so close you could hardly find Mom, though she's as tall as he is. I watched them from the stairs till I'd seen all I could handle.

In those first days I scrubbed out pens and hosed down the runs and cleaned up quite a lot of messes. We were well stocked with dog flesh, but the people before

11

had run a sloppy operation. Dad hadn't hired any part-time help yet, so I was it. I thought shoveling for him was better than decorating with Mom, which shows you where my head was.

One afternoon I was in the kennels taking caked grease off the gas rings with a wire brush. I had on rubber boots and gloves. My hair was up under a painter's cap. I was streaked all over with rancid grease. I looked great. Smelled good too.

A man was outside, talking to Dad, and they were already up at the pens looking at the dogs. Behind him was a big station wagon with wood grain. A boy was by the car, leaning back on the hood, on his elbows.

The man turned out to be Mr. Kettering. He wore riding boots and a tweed hacking jacket: the type who doesn't know much about dogs. For one thing, his station wagon was too clean. He took out a pipe to fiddle with while he talked. Dad was about twice his size. His work-shirt sleeves were rolled up above his elbows.

I suppose Mr. Kettering saw Dad's skull. I mean the tattoo of a skull on Dad's forearm. You can't miss it. Underneath are three tattooed letters: BTD. I never asked him about it. Like his limp it was just part of him.

When I was younger, I thought BTD were the initials of some girl, before Mom. I believe I pictured her as a Morgan Fairchild type. But then I figured the skull wasn't quite right for that.

"This is my girl, Chelsea," Dad said, waving me over. "She's starting school here this fall."

Lucy came bounding up. Did I mention Lucy was a dog? You don't make pets out of dogs you're training, so Lucy filled the pet position. She was a weimaraner with a terrible nose. She couldn't point an ostrich, and of course she was gun-shy. Weimaraners are supposed to have savage dispositions, but Lucy had never got the word. She was very sloppy-footed, but ladylike. It's possible she thought she was a poodle.

Anyway, Lucy came bounding up, and Mr. Kettering was calling Craig over, and he was the first person I met from Crestwood High School. He blew me away. He was wearing Reeboks, thick around his ankles, with big, loose socks and spotless white recycled pants and the preppiest golf shirt on earth. Even without the great face he'd have been a perfect picture of a golden boy.

"I'd like you to meet my son, Craig," Mr. Kettering said, and Craig froze. I saw that.

"My stepson, that is."

I figured girls don't have to shake hands, which was just as well considering my grease-slick rubber gloves. Then we were walking away together while Dad tried to explain to Mr. Kettering the difference between a Brittany spaniel and an English setter.

"This is the Pforzheimers' old place, isn't it?" Craig said.

I thought maybe his family had owned it at one time. There was ownership in his eyes when he surveyed the scene. But later I saw how Craig seemed to own everything he looked at.

"Yes," I said, "the Pforzheimers lived here, in the big house, of course."

"Is it still standing? My grandparents used to go to parties there."

So we walked in that direction. I hadn't been up

close to the main house before. It was at the other end of an overgrown grape arbor, and tall weeds tend to remind me of snakes. We took another way along a path where you could see most of the flagstones. I let him go ahead.

"Your stepfather in the market?" I said, looking for conversation.

"The stock market," he said over his shoulder.

"I mean in the market for a dog."

"He probably wouldn't mind a couple to lie at his feet on the Oriental in his den."

"A lot of people looking at hunting dogs really just want pets," I said.

"He wouldn't want a pet. He'd want a prop. Some little four-footed aristocrat to go with the color scheme."

I didn't exactly know what to make of that. Not liking your father, even a stepfather, was new to me.

"You don't like him?"

"You have to keep them guessing," he said. "You have to keep them off guard."

He lifted a low branch and held it up for me. "But no, my stepfather's not in the market for a dog. He just shops a lot. He went shopping once and bought my mother."

That was a little bewildering too.

"You and your father live here alone?" he asked me.

I wanted to say yes. A year younger and I would have. "Not exactly. My mom lives with us."

We crossed what used to be lawn, and the Pforzheimers' old house loomed over us. We'd come in from the side. The main drive to the house comes up

14

the other way from Artesia Avenue. Craig climbed the steps to the terrace by a post where an urn had probably been. He stood there surveying the world while I caught up with him, kicking through the grass just in case.

Lumber was nailed in big X's over the long windows, and the glass was out of all of them. You couldn't see anything inside, only the suggestion of things. It was dead silent except for the whirring of pigeons from somewhere deep in the house.

"Grandmother said one of the long rooms had a tile floor and that's where they danced." Craig ran his hand down the crumbling wall. "You know, saxophones and tuxedos—the whole thing."

"Not real," I said.

"Not really." Then he seemed to have seen enough, and we turned back the way we'd come.

"What year will you be in school?"

"Bottom of the barrel," I said. "Sophomore."

He grinned. It was just crooked enough, and he had a chipped tooth. It knocked me out. "Me too."

I couldn't believe it. I'd taken him for a junior at least. Still, it was pretty easy to talk to him. What did I have to lose? He'd never recognize me again. The way I looked, he probably couldn't tell which sex I was.

"What's Crestwood like?"

He turned up his hands. "Like junior high, with cars. Some of us have gone all the way through from first grade together."

I could grasp that all right. His group, the best bunch. They're in every school, and you know every-

15

thing about them, but you never really know them unless you're one of them.

"Have you changed schools before?" he asked, almost reading my mind.

"Three or four times. My last school was in a college town where my mom was finishing up her graduate degree."

Me volunteering information about Mom? I must have been carried away, but I didn't think it mattered. I figured he hadn't even caught my name.

We were nearly back to the kennels, and Mr. Kettering was in the station wagon, tapping the horn. Lucy was having a fit, leaping around. She chased cars, of course. Craig was walking away. "See you, Chelsea," he said.

"Ugly kid, wasn't he?" Dad said as the station wagon eased away. "Crazy about you, though." He slewed an eye around to me. "When the rest of the boys down at the high school get a look at you, I'll have my work cut out for me. They'll be dropping out of trees around here. They'll be barking louder than the dogs. Have to turn the hounds on them."

"Dad, give me a break."

But he gave me a one-armed hug instead, and Lucy came up on his other side, wanting hers.

There's only one other thing I remember before school started. One hot night Dad had gone out somewhere in the truck, and I was up in my room. Being on a different floor from Mom seemed to soothe me.

I don't remember what I was doing. I sure wasn't

calling anybody up, because I didn't have a phone of my own and I didn't know anybody to call. I guess I was just up there locked into my Walkman, replacing reality.

It was late when I heard the dogs start up. Maybe I heard Dad's truck coming back. After a minute there was a thundering sound, like somebody pounding on the door downstairs. I freed one ear from the Walkman, though I didn't hear anything more.

But I went out to the stairs and halfway down. In the light from the kitchen I saw the front door standing open. Mom was there, and Dad was on the threshold with the dark behind him. They seemed to move in slow motion. Dad's big hand came up to clutch at the door frame, holding on.

Then he fell into the room, like a tree. I thought he'd break through the floor. Mom couldn't catch him or cushion his fall. She went down on one knee beside him. I heard a sob, and it was terrible because it was Dad.

"One drink," he said.

"That's all it takes." Mom had her arm around his shoulder, but she couldn't begin to lift him. I guess she was holding him. His face showed in the kitchen light. It was wet, blurred.

"You know I don't want to worry you," he said, and his voice was blurred too.

"I know. I know that."

"You know I want to be here with you and not back there, in my mind."

"Yes," Mom said. "Yes."

He broke then and cried. She seemed to want him to

and cradled him. I didn't know his face. Since I didn't think they saw me, I started walking backward up the steps. In my room I tore off my clothes and got into my pajamas. I didn't go out to the bathroom to brush my teeth or anything. I didn't chance it.

When I thought I'd been in bed a long time, the door edged open, and Mom came in. We were both just shadows, but she could tell I was awake. She always can.

"Chelsea?"

I clamped my jaw tight and my eyes too. I hadn't seen anything. It never happened. This thing had happened with Dad before, other places, other times. But I wouldn't let it be real. Besides, whatever had hurt Dad must be her fault. She waited a long time before she went away. I suppose that next day was the start of school.

Chapter Three

I don't remember what I wore that first day—something safe. To give one of my hands something to do, I carried a blank notebook and walked all the way, carefully. It was only six blocks, but they were long, edge-of-town blocks, three of them without sidewalks. I must have been the only pedestrian at Crestwood. Town kids who couldn't drive were hand-delivered by parents.

Mom would have given me a ride. But even if nobody knew me, I didn't want to be seen in the car with her. It was her first day of work, and she was dressed for it. Nervous too. Usually she warmed up in the mornings with some at-home aerobics. I'd come in and find her with one long leg up on the kitchen counter, doing her stretches. But today she looked locked into her new work clothes: tight panty hose and shoes with little stacked heels, a precise bow at the neck of her blouse.

When I left the house, she was standing very still by the refrigerator, drinking tea, and the mug was jiggly in her hand.

On the way to school I worked up my big plan. So okay, it was an enormous school. I'd be a private citizen. I'd just go to classes and keep to myself. It'd probably be great for my grades. Adults can do that, can't they? They can just live their lives. They don't have to join or fit in or anything. They don't have to worry about who's watching. I figured I'd try for invisibility. It wasn't to be.

The first days were Registration in a gym big enough for zeppelins. Faculty sat at tables all around the walls. Once I found out which lines to stand in, I didn't mind how long they were. I liked it out there in the deafening middle of the gym floor, being anonymous near the end of the line. I'd have let people go ahead of me if anybody had asked.

Then I began noticing the guy standing ahead of me. He had lightish hair that stuck down from under a cap. A cigarette was wedged over his left ear. There was something cowboyish about him. He didn't have any hips to speak of, and his jeans were riding so low he looked like he might lose them. He was wearing a white undershirt with a lot of little holes in it.

When he turned around, our eyes were on the same level. He had his own ideas about designer labels. His long-billed plastic cap said CATERPILLAR TRACTOR across the front of it. His belt buckle read PETERBILT. I noticed the cowboy didn't shave yet.

"Hi," he said. "Want to get married?"

He grinned a big grin.

20

"Want to get engaged? Are you seeing anybody?"

He reached out and waved a hand in front of my eyes, to see if I was in there. "You live around here?"

"Everybody lives around here," I said in a low tone. Fortunately I'd left off the earrings. I hadn't done much with my hair except part it.

He planted his hands on where his hips should be and looked around. His eyes glazed over. They're deep blue—set a little too close together, but very blue. He happened to be looking at a line of six girls, probably juniors, all carrying fake Gucci bags, which were still big that year.

"Say, listen," he said, "where are we? Who are all these people? I haven't seen this many people since the last tractor pull. And how come they all look alike? Help, I'm being held prisoner on a clone farm."

What could I do? I had to stand in this line, so I just let him make his impression. Then he was noticing me again. "This is the right line for calculus, isn't it?"

So it seemed he hadn't finished making an impression.

"Not really," I said. "Not only that, but calculus is for people who've had algebra and geometry."

He looked stunned. "I guess that knocks me out of the ballpark. What line would this happen to be?"

I knew he knew, which made me feel like a nerd. "Elective minors," I said, not moving my lips much.

"And what are my choices there?" he wondered.

"Art, music, computer keyboarding, journalism, fashion merchandising, which only girls take probably, gourmet cooking, typing, marriage and the family, creative writing, and a couple more I forget."

21

He staggered back, smacking his cap. "You're on the verge of being a printout. How'd you know all that?"

"My—I just did. Anyway it's in the handbook they send out."

"I been having a lot of problems with the U.S. mails," he said. "I don't even get letters back from people I write to."

I decided to leave that line alone, but he was looking away again. He had the attention span of a gerbil. He caught sight of a girl standing in the next line over, not a very noticeable girl. She was reading a book while she waited and wore a shapeless black sweater over a denim skirt. Pretty drab, but no clone.

"Hey, Ruthie," he said. "How's it going?"

Looking up, she said, "Hi, Pod." Then she went back to her book, or tried to. She was making notes in the margin like she was in class already.

"That's Ruthie Baines. Her and me went to junior high together. But I don't know about these other people. They aren't too dis-tinguish-able. I mean, you can tell the preppies from the punkers, but even the sweats look like they set up a dress-code committee. You know what I mean?"

Not really.

"Say, listen," he—Pod—said, "I'd like you to meet Ruthie." He was sort of reaching out for her. "Hey, Ruthie, I'd like you to meet—" He blinked at me. I noticed his eyebrows, somewhat silky. "What'd you say your name is?"

I hadn't. "Chelsea."

"Is that a first name?"

"Chelsea Olinger."

"Well, then, Ruthie, this here is Chelsea Olinger. Chelsea, Ruthie Baines." He stood between us, out of line. If I hadn't been such a private citizen, I'd have been seriously embarrassed.

"Hi," I said to her, almost shrugging.

She'd rather have been reading her book, but she managed a nod. Then our line was moving forward, and Pod was walking backward.

"Pod Johnson's my name. Tenth grade's my game. Put her there."

Now I was supposed to shake his hand, which sure didn't seem like normal fifteen-year-old behavior to me. I had to shift my notebook around and take this loon's hand. He'd been working on his grip, but his hands weren't quite thorny enough for a cowboy's. "We didn't happen to go to junior high together, did we?" he said.

"Not unless you just blew in from four states over."

"Can't say I did. I'm just an old flop-eared country boy, comes into town for a little learning."

Very little probably, but by now he was at the front of the line, did another about-face, and picked his elective at random.

"Uh—gourmet cooking," he said.

Then it was my turn. "Creative writing," I said, and signed the sheet.

But now Pod was back. He'd never left. Planting both hands on the table, he said to the teacher, "I changed my mind. Put me down for creative whatever." Then he followed me up the line. I'd have walked faster, but ahead of me the lines were opening

23

up. Somebody was walking across them, and the crowds parted to let him pass.

It was Craig Kettering with three guys a lot like him coming along behind. You wouldn't have taken him for a first-day sophomore. He knew exactly where he was. And he looked better than before. The cuffs of his striped dress shirt were turned back. His hands were free to reach out and touch people, make contact. He nodded to a few of them.

He was coming past me, seeing me. "How's it going, Chelsea?" I saw the chipped tooth again when he smiled, and then he was gone. Pod was next to me now. He gave me a look like he hadn't really seen me before.

We stumbled through Registration and got our four majors and two minors plus PE into the computer. Then we were divided into homerooms. At Crestwood they're called advisories, but they're homerooms. For those ten minutes every morning we had a paraprofessional instead of a real teacher. Everybody called paraprofessionals "narcs" that year, which I didn't even understand. But the rumor was that they were actually undercover agents looking for controlled substances: pot in lockers, pills in purses. I never saw a shakedown, but in tenth grade you like rumors better than the truth anyway. I don't even remember our narc's name. She was supposed to take attendance, which wasn't easy, since people kept drifting in for the entire ten minutes.

Pod Johnson was in my advisory. It took him a while to amble down the aisle because he walked like a cowboy too. That first day he just happened to swing into the seat ahead of mine.

"Olinger, comma, Chelsea, am I right?" He seemed to be able to turn his head completely around like that girl in *The Exorcist.*

He gave me a blank look. "Hey, wait a minute, are you the same girl in the Registration line?"

And I fell for it. I thought he really didn't recognize me and I said the dumbest thing of my career.

"I'm not as tall sitting down."

He blinked. "Most people aren't."

Then he decided to put me in the picture by telling me about everybody in advisory, when I didn't even want to know him. Pod shifted sideways with his feet in the aisle.

"That's Megan Forrester just coming in the door. In seventh grade she was the girl with the biggest—and that girl with her who looks like an armadillo, that's Tammy Shellabarger." Pod warmed to the task. "And that guy at the front of the next row, the one whose ears don't match? That's Bobby Ray Hetherington. And behind him is Wes Miller, then Ruthie Baines, who you already met, then Gretchen—"

"Pod," I said, "am I going to go through the rest of high school with you right in front of me, spilling your guts?"

He scratched up under his cap, a habit. "Not a bad idea," he said. "Glad you suggested it. I wouldn't have had the nerve."

Then something happened that changed everything. I'd been keeping an eye out for Craig Kettering, but he turned out to be in a different advisory. Instead, this girl came in.

Other girls dash in, clutching their books, or try to be in the middle of a crowd. This one wasn't like that. She stopped just inside the door. She'd been talking to another girl just behind her, and her head was still back, listening. Then she glanced around. The room went quiet, even the boys. Especially the boys.

It wasn't her looks, which were great. It wasn't even her clothes, which you didn't notice. She didn't even look particularly mature, which is a big thing in tenth grade. She wouldn't have passed for a senior, and something about her said she didn't want to. She walked across the room with the other girl following. They passed in front of the narc, who noticed her too.

When she got over by the windows, she did a perfect thing. She pulled a desk out of line and angled it halfway toward the rest of us. Then she sat down in a fluid kind of move. The other girl took the desk nearest her. They exchanged another word or two, like they might be anywhere, like it wasn't particularly important that they were in school.

Then she smiled. I don't know at what. Maybe nothing, and she had braces. They glinted. Somehow that was the final touch. She had braces and she didn't care. They looked great on her—jewelry for the mouth.

Strangely enough, Pod didn't say anything until I poked him. "What's that girl's name?"

"The dark-headed one is Lauren Sperling."

"Not her. The other one."

"That would be Ashley Packard."

"And who is she?"

26

"Words wouldn't express it."

"Try."

Pod hunched his shoulders—bare, of course. He was wearing one of his undershirts. "Ashley's in charge."

I believed him. I kept looking at Ashley Packard and saw her as a little girl entering kindergarten all those years ago. I saw she'd been in charge from the first day she set foot in the sandbox.

"And Craig Kettering belongs to her," I said so Pod could hear.

"If you know everything already, why ask me?" He sounded downright cranky.

But I hadn't known anything. I was an outsider. Suddenly I didn't want to be one. It must have been the way the room was bright now, and kind of promising. I didn't want to be a private citizen. I wanted to—I don't know what. I really wanted to be in this school.

I wanted to be there breathing the same air as Craig Kettering and Ashley Packard. I wanted to settle in here and make a life, I guess. I decided I could even put up with being directly behind Pod Johnson with his head on backward. I tell you what I wanted. I wanted to have a lot of fun. It was my new plan.

27

Chapter Four

But it was like flipping on TV in the middle of this long complicated show with a huge cast. Weeks went by, and I wasn't finding a foothold. I was drowning in strangers and fell back on my earlier plan, the private-citizen one, without wanting to. I watched other people living.

The new seniors moved through the halls like gods and goddesses. They were free to leave school whenever they didn't have classes, took reduced loads because they'd fulfilled a lot of requirements, cut out early for part-time jobs they didn't have. They haunted their own cars out in the parking lot and their own private lounge in the Activities Wing. It was originally a smoking lounge for anybody with a note from parents saying they could smoke. But the lounge was now a senior tradition, and all other smokers had to stand out in a field across the street.

The juniors ran everything, or thought they did.

29

They took over Student Alliance, which is what Crestwood calls student council, and they made a lot of announcements.

Even the bulletin boards were baffling: all curly with notices about college admissions and study abroad and pre-SAT seminars and all kinds of clubs you could join. The bulletin boards bristled with warnings too—against drugs and alcohol and unsafe sex, all kinds of things nobody read.

One major thing they do at Crestwood is decorate lockers. It's this big honor. For your birthday your friends, if you have any, always cover your locker door with twisted crepe paper and silver balloons and a lot of cuteness. Girls do this for girls. Girls do this for their boyfriends, or even friends of their boyfriends.

The football team got all their lockers decorated by the Pep Squad. On the Friday before every game the halls were full of cheerleaders in little pleated skirts, clustered around some quarterback's locker, Scotch-taping it all over with his number and the school colors (green and gold) and screaming. It was deafening.

Craig Kettering wasn't in any of my classes. I figured any class he was in filled up because he was in it. Ashley Packard was in creative writing, and so was Pod, of course. But we sat in a circle in there, so he wasn't in front of me, and Ashley sat by herself. Biology was a bunch of complete strangers. And though I should have taken geometry, I sleazed out with general math. *Sleaze* was another big word that year.

Not knowing what I was doing, I picked chorus for my other elective. What I didn't know was that all the right guys were in computer keyboarding and all the right girls were in fashion merchandising. Ashley Packard was in fashion merchandising.

Everybody's elective-of-choice was drivers' ed, because we were all counting the days till we turned sixteen and could get licenses. But that class was filled up with people who'd been able to preregister in the summer, or sometime before I even got here. Figures.

In advisory they announced the winning slate of officers for Sophomore Class Council. I was so out of it that the election itself got right by me. I didn't know who the president and vice-president were when they named them. I poked Pod.

"I can't believe Craig isn't president and Ashley vice-president, or vice versa."

Pod shrugged and mumbled something.

"What?"

"They're above it," he said.

I didn't know whether he was being sarcastic or not. I believed it. Let other people run meetings and bang gavels and take notes. Ashley and Craig didn't need that.

The big event of the semester was already happening. It started slow, but it gathered a lot of momentum. Somebody was sleazing the sacred seniors. A few people went to their cars during free period and found some kind of disgusting slime smeared all over their steering wheels. This led to the air being let out of some tires. It didn't take long to see the pattern. All the cars belonged to seniors.

Weird little false messages found their way onto the PA. One of the assistant principals reads morning announcements from a printout, and he himself informed

31

the seniors that anybody thinking about applying to Harvard, Stanford, Baylor, University of Miami, TCU, Colorado, and I forget where else should report to the gym right after fourth period.

It was a big hoax, and not the assistant principal's fault. He just reads what's put in front of him. Hardly a senior was in fifth-period class. They were all down milling around in the gym without a college rep in sight. The coaches went crazy.

Then *Twilight Zone* type things began to happen in the senior lounge. Somebody got in there and practically wallpapered the place with copies of a poster that read,

SMOKING AND CONSUMING ALCOHOLIC
BEVERAGES DURING PREGNANCY CAN
RESULT IN BIRTH DEFECTS

And nobody could figure out how anybody had the time for this job, because the seniors are hardly ever out of the place. Except for before first period when it's quiet as a tomb.

One day twenty-eight pizzas were delivered to the lounge. This was fine with the seniors, except they hadn't ordered them and didn't have enough class solidarity to raise the money to pay the pizza man. Another day the lounge loudspeaker suddenly blared:

"Seniors! Report to room 348 to have your yearbook pictures taken, *now.*"

It was over so fast nobody recognized the voice. A lot of senior girls started screaming because their hair was a mess. No pictures were being taken, of course, and worse yet, there is no room 348.

There were a lot of incidents, coming closer together. People started calling the mysterious forces Gremlins, and the seniors were getting paranoid. They weren't responding to real announcements.

"Who's doing it, Pod?" I figured he'd have a theory.

But he just swiveled his head around and gave me an evil look with his close-together eyes. "Why not just kick back and enjoy it?" he said. "It works for me."

I suppose I was enjoying it. "But who's behind it?"

"I bet if you thought about it real hard, Chelsea, you could reason it out." Then he squinted at me to see how smart I was, so I just looked somewhere else.

One day things went too far. We were getting into basketball season, and somebody decorated Ty Hollister's locker, early one Friday morning. It wasn't the Pep Squad.

Even off the court Ty was a star center: six foot five and gorgeous, even modest, considering. Films were made of his fall-away jump shot, and colleges came in Learjets, trying to recruit him. He had to have an unlisted phone number for what little privacy he could get. The Pep Squad worked up a cheer just for him:

Lottsa teams run lukewarm
Lottsa teams run hot
Crestwood has Ty Hollister
Who do you think you've got?

Not a great cheer, but all his.

The morning Ty's locker was decorated was the day before the game with El Monte High School, our deadliest rivals. They never give us any real competition. In

33

fact they can't win much but a coin toss. But they're on the other side of town, so they're our deadliest rivals.

When the Pep Squad arrived with their crepe paper and balloons, they found Ty's locker completely draped with black cloth, pulled tight and sort of coffin-shaped. Stretched across it from all four corners was this large white elastic X, which turned out to be a jockstrap. On the pouch of it, right in the middle of the locker door, was a neatly lettered little scoreboard predicting the outcome of the game:

El Monte   104
Crestwood   36

The Pep Squad took it hard. A lot of them just stood there in their little skirts and cried. Shar Watson, head cheerleader, said, "This grosses me out so seriously I could, like, spit." A crowd gathered, of course.

It was close to sacrilegious. Just the idea that El Monte could whip us was outrageous enough. Sleazing Ty Hollister's locker broke new records. If they'd had any sense, the Pep Squaders would have ripped the stuff down and replaced it fast with their green and gold. But they didn't. They drew a crowd to watch them grossing out.

It changed the complexion of the pep rally that afternoon. By then everybody knew about Ty's locker, and the seniors were taking it so personally that most of them stayed in school the whole day.

Finally they about decided to rise above it, and the entire school turned out for the rally. Everybody was there, including the people who hang out in the art department and people you only see in chorus. Pod sat with me in the sophomore section, or maybe I sat with him. Nobody quite knows the words to the fight song, but we all hummed loud, and the band sounded good. When it came to the cheers, Shar's Pep Squaders gave their all. Ty Hollister always got a standing ovation when he came on the stage suited up. That day people stood on their chairs, including a few teachers.

"That's what we like to see," the principal said, vaulting up on the stage. "This is the true Crestwood spirit with nothing negative about it!"

The head basketball coach was up there, too, pretty red in the face and getting redder.

"Coach is medium steamed," Pod remarked.

Ahead of his turn the coach grabbed the microphone and said, "I want to believe a bunch of dirtbags from El Monte got into this school and tried to rub our noses in it. I want to believe it, but I don't. I think it was an inside job, because there's a lot of dead wood in this school." He parked his fists on his big hips and scanned out across us. "There's a lot of dead wood out there, and you know who you are."

Pod's head was way down and he was grinning big. Finally the coach finished up and threw his cap on the floor. We had the fight song again.

When we got up to leave, Pod said, "It's about time for him to break cover. This is about as far as he's going to go."

"What are you talking about?" I said. "Who?" But he let a bunch of people get between us, and we were separated.

We whipped El Monte 94 to 58, but a lot of people's feathers were still ruffled. They said the Gremlins had narrowed the margin. They said we should have trounced El Monte by at least fifty points. It's a good thing Ty Hollister didn't get a stress fracture or something during the game. If that had happened, there'd have been people out for Gremlin blood.

They were caught, but it was a couple of weeks later. The rumor of a Gremlin bust started vibing through the school early one morning. But there were several versions. As near as anybody could tell, one or more Gremlins were caught posting a bogus notice somewhere, telling all the seniors to pick up their class rings in the attendance office, *now*. Either that or something else. Nobody was sure. Nobody was sure who they were, either, though plenty of people claimed to. We talked about it through every class until the teachers went buggy.

A lot of names were named, nobody too interesting —the usual suspects. Then around lunch Spence Whitfield's name came up. That drew attention to our class, because he was captain of the tenth-grade tennis team. Nobody believed it except the seniors, who announced that they'd had their eyes on the sophomores all along because it was the kind of stuff we'd pull.

By fifth period Gil Esterbrook's name was going the rounds, maybe because he's in with Spence Whitfield. So that's why people were starting to mention Mark Gardner by sixth period, because wherever Spence and Gil are, Mark is.

By seventh period a sudden silence descended. Spence and Gil and Mark never made a move without their leader. Their leader was Craig Kettering.

Pod just grinned. When I asked him why, he'd only say that the whole deal was "inevitable."

Chapter Five

I kept poking Pod in advisory.

"What's so inevitable about it? I can't even believe they'd do that kind of thing *and* get caught. Craig and his guys are too cool. They've got a reputation."

"Keep thinkin', Chelsea," he said over his shoulder. "You'll get there."

But I didn't see how, and he knew it. Whenever he speaks without his country-boy twang, you know he means business. "Look, Chelsea, you weren't here last year for ninth grade when Craig was top man. He was the absolute ayatollah of junior high, okay?"

I nodded.

"And what is he now? A sophomore. And who are the big guns around here?"

". . . Seniors."

"Right. Craig needed to make his mark and early. Being president of the sophomore class wouldn't cut it.

Who cares? He needed to put this school in his pocket from day one, and he did. Notice they were just pranks, nothing critical. He wouldn't get booted out of school even if he wasn't Craig Kettering. It wasn't serious. It was just—show business. And the seniors were right about us. It's the type of stunt sophomores like. Being a Gremlin's a little too immature for Craig, but it's just about right for the rest of the class. He's still our hero, and now the whole school knows him too. He wins twice."

I found that reasoning somewhat impressive. "I don't know," I said. "Maybe."

But now Ashley was coming in, looking as usual. A few girls who wanted in with her and weren't said things like "It can't be true about Craig, and we're really destroyed, and we know how you must be feeling," et cetera.

Ashley only smiled in a neutral way and went over to her special seat, and it was Dina Westervelt's day to sit nearest her.

You didn't see Ashley and Craig together much around school. There are couples hanging all over each other just to prove something. But Ashley and Craig didn't need that. You'd see her around his locker sometimes and him around hers. But it was like they were these two people, not kids at all, not locked up here like the rest of us. And you wouldn't see them leaving together after school. We weren't old enough to drive yet, and it didn't give quite the right image to be seen walking much. They both seemed so mature to me, especially Ashley, that it made me kind of dizzy.

There's a thing at Crestwood, new that year, called ISS—"In-School Suspension." That's where they put you to serve your sentence during the school day. You have to go there if they've caught you breaking a major rule more than ten times or getting incorrigible or, in the case of Craig and his guys, being Gremlins.

ISS is supposed to isolate some of the high-spirited hyperactives and the drug-dazed and their dealers. They even had a senior in there once, for a day. It was Raleigh Kornbluth, but only because he'd tried to drive a Porsche through the window wall of the cafeteria. Now they had Spence, Gil, Mark, and Craig.

A guidance counselor was in charge to keep them calm and to oversee the schoolwork teachers sent to them. They had to spend every day there, segregated, even during Advisory and lunch. For PE they did aerobics in the aisle beside their desks.

The sentence Craig and his Gremlins drew was determined by Student Alliance. The senior reps came up with two weeks of ISS, another four of community service, and a public apology. The sophomore reps thought a morning of ISS should do it, along with a vote of thanks to the Gremlins for showing class spirit. The juniors worked out a compromise for a week of ISS and then let's forget about the whole thing.

ISS was about half a joke. People said it had padded walls and they didn't let you have sharp objects in there. But it was an ordinary classroom, 212. The guidance counselor in charge of it was Miss Larrimore. She was said to be incredibly tough, like a warden, but that was just your typical paranoia. Doing time in ISS didn't even hurt your reputation much, if you had one. In a few cases it helped.

Life slowed down in the week the Gremlins were separated from society. The seniors went back to being seniors, and the sophomores were leaderless. Still, Craig in exile looked better than ever. He and his Gremlins wouldn't eat the cafeteria food sent over to them because it got cold. Craig started carrying a Thermos full of some power drink for lunch. So a lot of sophomore guys began bringing Thermoses full of something or other to drink in the cafeteria. But life slowed down.

Then suddenly something wonderful happened. I thought it was a miracle because it happened to me. Surprisingly, it was in creative writing.

At the beginning of the year I thought I'd made another of my mistakes by electing creative writing, even though Ashley Packard was in it. It was a smaller group than a regular class, with some juniors in it, so it was different. I thought for a while it was too different.

Everybody was pretty concerned about the teacher, Mr. Mallory. He was new and English—British English, here in this country for a year on a foreign exchange. People thought he might be hard because he wasn't too young and he wore a suit. Also he was foreign.

Somebody told him that he talked so funny that we might not be able to understand what he was saying.

"Oh, think nothing of it," he said. "I only catch the odd word from you lot myself. I rather imagine we'll be able to rub along together."

40

A lot of people didn't even follow that, but Pod was grinning like a jack-o'-lantern.

Then a junior girl, wanting to lay down some ground rules, said, "Since this is *creative* writing, we're really going to be writing from our hearts, you know? So I don't think we ought to be, like, held back. Like with grades."

Mr. Mallory smiled a private smile and said, "So it's true what I've heard about American students."

Pod grinned even wider.

People couldn't understand why we had to learn new vocabulary and keep going back to grammar in a creative writing class, especially an elective minor. The junior girl dealt with it by dropping the course.

We were also worried we'd have to write according to certain forms, like sonnets or something. But Mr. Mallory wasn't that way. He didn't care what we wrote as long as we kept at it. The only catch was that he wanted us to read some of our things out loud. Nobody liked the sound of that, but it was either that or grades on everything. Pod spent the early days being Pod. All of his poetry was more or less rhymed and went:

> *Gimme my red-eye gravy, my Coors, and my grits*
> *And a day in the saddle till it hurts where I sits.*

He kept it up and refined it only a little. But Mr. Mallory just said that Pod's poetry "marched in a picturesquely primitive tradition of American folklore." Pod took that kindly and spent a few weeks thinking about going country-and-western on lyrics for Nashville. In tenth grade he always had to establish his cowboy image before he could get anything else done.

41

I didn't know what to write about. I sure wasn't going to write about myself if I might have to read it out loud. But writing something or other every day got me into a rhythm. Mr. Mallory said if we got writer's block, we should make lists of vocabulary words we could draw on later. I made a lot of lists.

I never tried poetry. Just for myself I jotted some notes on the growing Gremlin Mystery and other things happening around school, things I'd look back on later. Instead of just watching other people live, I began writing about them, and that was the way I was living.

Then one day Ashley read a poem. She'd been quiet in class. She didn't have one of the girls in her group with her, and so she sat there alone, composed. That, too, seemed incredibly mature to me. I watched her when we were supposed to be writing. She'd look up from her notebook a lot, and the top of her pen just grazed her lips as she gazed out the window with leafy patterns on her face. She never seemed to write much. In fact she drew a lot of pictures in margins. But one day she read a poem, just sitting there at her desk. She had a honey-soft voice, younger than her words:

> If time is a river,
> then I'm on the shore,
> on a sandbar,
> soft but solid.
>
> I feel the sun on my shoulders,
> the sand between my toes;
> I stand still
> while time flows past me.

42

I let it, turning my face
back to somewhere safer:
childhood, maybe,
or earlier still.

Mr. Mallory's eyebrows were usually high on his forehead, but they went higher after Ashley's poem. The room was really quiet, even juniors. Nobody could think of a criticism. I suppose we were all still seeing the images in the poem.

I wanted to say something—that hearing the poem was like looking through a window. It let you see inside Ashley to that touch of sadness and uncertainty I wouldn't have believed was there. It made her more real, and better. I couldn't have said that. It was the kind of thing girls said when they wanted to be in with her.

Finally Mr. Mallory spoke. "Have you any more?"

Ashley smiled; looked down. "I don't know. Sometimes when I think a poem's there, it isn't."

After that day creative writing was my favorite class. I even liked it entirely through Pod's Nashville period and all those heartbreaking love songs that began,

All my women are hard-hearted,
A whole lot more cold than hot,
I give 'em my heart on a platter of gold,
And they give me diddledy-squat.

Then, one day before class started, the miracle happened. It was that week the Gremlins were in ISS. I was scribbling in my notebook, and somebody sat down

43

next to me. I glanced up and it was Ashley. I'd never seen her that close. I must have looked—surprised.

"Well, Chelsea, what do you think of the class?" She put her head on one side and waited, like she really wanted to know.

I nodded, which meant I liked it or something. I was trying to believe she actually knew my name.

"So do I," she said. "I wasn't sure at first, but it seems to be working out."

My tongue was completely dead in my mouth. Pod ambled in, saw who was sitting next to me, stopped dead, and keeled sideways into a seat.

"Why don't you ever read anything in class?" Ashley was saying. To me. "Mallory's going to get around to you sooner or later. Why don't you beat him to it?"

". . . I never have anything good enough."

For a second I wondered what Ashley wanted from me, so I must have been in shock.

"Tell you what," she said. "Read something, and I'll back you up. You know—positive criticism or maybe just praise." She smiled and her braces winked. At me?

"Oh, I . . . maybe." Then I pulled myself together. "I should have backed you up," I said. "You didn't need it, but I wanted to say how great your poem was. Everybody's waiting for another one from you."

"So am I," she said, smiling.

Mr. Mallory came in, and Ashley slipped out of the seat next to mine. "See you later," she said. "You know what we ought to do?"

We? She was standing there by my desk, and we were just these two people talking, as if the room wasn't there.

44

"We ought to get together," she said. "I mean, we've got all of high school ahead of us, and we ought to get organized. If you don't have anything better to do, why not come over after school?"

"Where?"

"My house." Then she walked across the room to her seat by the window, just slightly apart from the circle. I wasn't sure it had happened. But I read something out loud that day while I was still in an altered state. I didn't think it was good enough, but I read this thing about dogs. At least I know something about them. It wasn't about Lucy, because that would have been sloppy and sentimental, like Lucy. I wrote about the business of raising pointers, so in a way I was writing about Dad without actually mentioning him. I came pretty close. Some people say you have to raise pointers as workers, machines even. You aren't supposed to show them any affection. But Dad isn't like that with them, and I worked that in.

I went through the process, how it takes three years before they're ready to hunt and what goes into training them. In an earlier draft I'd told the whole thing from the growing puppy's viewpoint, but fortunately I'd junked that. When I started reading, it didn't sound so bad, and my voice didn't wobble much. It occurred to me that I might even have a small writing talent.

It's always too quiet after people read to the class. Then Ashley spoke and everybody turned to her. "It works," she said. "It's real. You can smell it, and it smells good."

Somehow that was the perfect thing to say. Then Pod of all people had to put his two cents' worth in. "I agree

45

with Ashley," he said as if they were well-known pals. "But it needs more. Background information or something."

I wanted to fly across the room and whap him on the Caterpillar cap with my notebook.

"That's my response too," Mr. Mallory said. Men, I thought. They stick together. They're animals. "Tell us, Chelsea, how do you know about the canine world?"

I didn't want them to know. I didn't want Ashley to know that all my dad does is train dogs. It was the first time I'd been embarrassed that he isn't . . . somebody else. I fought it. I couldn't lie; at least I didn't. I told them my dad trains hunting dogs, that it's a specialized skill and needs patience and a lot of other things. I laid out that part of my life and let them look.

Ashley listened, and I wondered if I was closing a door on myself. But she was leaning forward, interested. The top of her pen was grazing her lips. Pod was interested, too, in his way. He was draped in his seat, and his beady eyes were on me.

It was a good day, the best I'd had. At that age you don't quibble with miracles. I went over to Ashley's house that afternoon. I went there as often as she invited me, until I'd almost forgotten who I'd been.

Chapter Six

Because Ashley Packard's house is nearly next door to Los Alamitos Country Club, you wouldn't think it needed a swimming pool. But it has one, heated. Even when the weather got gusty and winterish, you could lounge around the pool in a sheltered courtyard. Besides, there seemed to be a little circle of sunlight around Ashley.

When we came into the house that first day, she lingered at the door to a long living room. A woman was sitting in there, reading a magazine, *Vogue,* but she stood up. She was thin as a reed, in white slacks and a blue silk blouse. Her smile was quicker than Ashley's.

"This is Chelsea," Ashley said from the hall, "Chelsea Olinger, from school."

And while I was mumbling something, Ashley's hand closed over my wrist.

The woman took a half step forward but stopped.

Maybe the coffee table was in her way. It was big and low with sculpture on it and a bowl of out-of-season tulips. Ashley drew me on toward the French doors that led out to the courtyard. Behind us the woman was saying, "I'll have something sent out to you."

"No, don't," Ashley called back. "We'll go to the kitchen ourselves."

She swerved through a swinging door, and we were in the kitchen, which was several rooms. A woman in a white uniform was at a counter doing something with a blender. She was a maid, and I had a strange little fantasy. Wouldn't it be funny if Ashley was the maid's daughter? What if she was this Cinderella who really lived in the kitchen and came out of it to turn into a butterfly at school every day? Somehow it was comforting. It was also a fantasy.

"Mabel, we're starved. What can you do for us?"

The maid—Mabel—looked up. "How about fruit for your figures and brownies and spiced tea?"

So Ashley took a tray from a place where they were all shelved according to size, and a linen tea cloth, and arranged things on it. It wasn't like grabbing a half bag of Doritos on your way to the TV set.

Out by the pool we sat on long lounge chairs. There were chrysanthemums all around us in autumn colors. We talked about school, Ashley did, and I was all ears.

"It's your life," she said, "but if I were you I wouldn't get too clubby at Crestwood. Some people are joiners, but after you've spent all that time on activities, what have you got?"

I didn't know, but I said, "What about college? Don't they look at your activities when you get ready to ap-

48

ply?" I knew I wanted to go to college. We'd lived in a college town, Bloomington, while Mom was in grad school. The college kids were the ones I'd looked up to, before Ashley.

"College?" Her eyes went a little out of focus. "I wouldn't get too crazed about that yet if I were you." And she returned us to the present, where she was in charge. "Actually, I think this is the point where we start talking about boys."

"Except I don't know any boys."

"Well, you more or less know Craig. Everybody does. He's made sure of that."

I decided to chance it. "How long have you two been —an item?"

She has gray eyes with grayer flecks in them. They crinkle up when she smiles a certain way. "I don't even remember when Craig wasn't there. And by the way, he never had an awkward age. His voice changed conveniently over the summer after seventh grade, and if he's ever had a zit, it's where you can't see it."

We grinned at each other, like old friends. "You never had an awkward age either," I said. "I bet you didn't."

"I don't know," she said. "It's easier to tell about other people."

That, too, impressed me. "Anyway, you two are an item now."

"Whatever that means," she said. "It's not exactly like kissing your brother, but I don't know. There's still time, and why rush things? I'm not sure I believe in happy endings." Ashley ran a hand through her hair. She was a lot better blonde than I was, though later I

49

did something about that. "You know," she said, "it could be that all those Candlelight Romances are actually fiction."

She smiled a somewhat wicked smile, and I thought she was so mature I'd soon stop understanding a word she said. She jiggled the ice in her glass. "Sometimes I think Craig and I both better end up with two other people. Maybe two people who haven't always had everything they wanted."

I thought she was amazing, but she brought me back to earth by saying, "And on the subject of boys, you know Pod Johnson."

"Oh, well, Pod," I said. "Pod knows everybody. On the first day of Registration he was all for introducing me around and got as far as Ruth Baines."

"Who?" Ashley said.

"You know, Ruth Baines in advisory. Kind of intense, wears glasses. You all went to junior high together."

Ashley's brow got little furrows in it. "I'm not sure," she said.

I didn't believe her. She had to know who Ruth Baines was, at least from a distance. But then I just thought I wasn't describing her right, or something.

The French doors opened, and the tall woman in blue and white was coming toward us. "Ah," Ashley said. "Celia."

Calling your mother Celia? I was blown totally away. She—Celia—came over to us and hovered. She was great-looking, with a year-round tan, but she had little crow's-feet fanning out from her eyes and worry lines around her mouth. "Am I intruding?"

"Not at all," Ashley said, very woman-to-woman.

50

"We'd just finished up about boys and were getting to the main business." She nodded to a chair. It was a stiff iron one by the umbrella table, and Celia edged onto it.

"I was just going to tell Chelsea about the St. Joseph's Hospital Junior Board in case she hasn't heard about it yet."

I shook my head.

"It's a charity thing and supposed to be a big deal. It involves girls from schools all over the city, so it's not just a Crestwood activity. Girls from three or four of the best high schools get appointed to the Junior Board. It's fun, and I've had my eye on it. They have a big fashion show in June. The stores loan the clothes, really good stores like Montaldo's, and we wear them. Sort of frivolous, but all for a good cause."

I'd never been to a fashion show, but I could picture Ashley modeling: coming down a runway in something completely grown up. Celia was seeing that too. "It sounds nice," she said. "I never—it sounds nice."

"And I got appointed from our class," Ashley said. "Having two aunts and an old family friend on the Senior Board didn't hurt my chances much."

Celia just listened.

"They need another girl from Crestwood to do some modeling," Ashley said, "and I pick Chelsea."

Who? "Me?" A brownie jumped out of my lap. I left a puddle of spiced tea on the terrace.

"That's nice," Celia said, faintly.

"Why would you want me?" I said. "I can't be a model. I don't even have a figure. I don't want to be a model."

But I did. All of a sudden I wanted to be a model bad.

51

Models don't have figures, and they're all too tall. I was a natural. I might even take it up professionally.

"I can't do that, Ashley. Anyway, you don't want me. Why not ask Lauren Sperling?"

That was Ashley's opportunity to betray one of her most faithful sidekicks, the almost beautiful Lauren Sperling. This was the time for her to point out that Lauren couldn't make it down the runway—that her knees looked at each other—that she limped and was secretly retarded.

"I thought about Lauren, but she's going to be big in Girls' Club at Crestwood. She's basically pretty ambitious, and if she starts turning up on every board and doing everything, they won't take her seriously. She's gunning for president of GC by junior year, and she'll have to concentrate on that."

My mind wandered among Ashley's friends, taking names. "Well, but what about Meredith Hastings?"

"Meredith dances," Ashley said. "In fact her mother's a founder of Dance Theater. Meredith goes to class every day and doesn't have time."

Landis Williamson's so beautiful that I skipped over her. "Dina Westervelt?"

"Her father's about to be appointed under secretary of something-or-other. You never know when Dina will have to be in Washington. Besides, she's only five feet tall. She'd look like a gnome up there on the runway, and she knows it. She'd look like Mary Lou Retton wearing her mother's clothes."

I gave up and sat there panting lightly. This whole world they lived in was too complicated. I'd never figure it out. I should be home grooming dogs with Dad where I'd be safe. And the whole time I kept seeing myself coming down the runway, in something from Montaldo's.

I didn't refuse. Who'd refuse Ashley? It was time to go, getting late. I'd never been anywhere after school. She walked me back through the house, leaving Celia by the pool. In the front hall was a tall mirror in a gold frame. She never even glanced at herself.

"Well, thanks," I said. ". . . I really enjoyed meeting your mother."

"My what?" Ashley swallowed a smile. "Celia's not my mother, or anybody's. She's a 'friend' of my father. Get it?"

Almost. "You mean your own mother—"

"Gone," Ashley said. "Quite a while ago. She lives in L.A. I see her in the summers. It's enough. At our age who wants a mother?"

Exactly.

I left in a daze. I could barely find my way home.

When I got there, I didn't know the place. Lucy came bounding up, looking a lot like herself, but the house was smaller than it had been that morning, tacky. The kitchen was just an alcove. Mom was already home, at the kitchen table bent over work: a big pile of catalogs she was studying. She still had on her work clothes except for shoes. I'd trained her never to ask me where I'd been, even when I hadn't been anywhere.

Still, she wondered, glancing up at the clock. I thought of freezing her out. Old habits die hard. But I wanted to be different now, not me at all. Because I'd been to Ashley's, and so this was the first day of the rest of my life. "I've been over at Ashley Packard's." I

53

didn't sound casual about it. That would have been going too far.

"Oh," Mom said. "Why? I mean—oh."

We'd been getting along okay all fall, better than I'd expected. I'd spent my at-home time divided mainly between working in the kennels and being in my room.

In October there'd been Open School Night, when the parents could meet the teachers. "At least spare me that," I'd said, and she did. Dad kept out of all arguments, which was another point in his favor. Mom talked to him about her job a lot, and I'd sit at the top of the stairs, listening out of sight.

But now I'd been at Ashley's. "Do you want to cut my hair this weekend?" I asked Mom, making it sound like this treat I was offering her. She's good at cutting hair. She cuts Dad's. She even lines up mirrors behind her and cuts her own. It didn't dawn on me that she did it to save money. I thought of it as her hobby.

"It's a deal," she said. "Your usual or something new?"

"I don't know."

"How about a lot shorter, just down to the tip of the ear, with a little more fullness." She was describing Ashley's hair, accurately.

"Maybe. I don't know."

"Why not?" she said. "It'll look just as good on you as it does on her. Maybe better."

I hated it when Mom read my mind. It was pushy and witchy. I started to freeze her out. Then Dad loomed in.

"Where's my helper been all this time?"

I turned to him, which was always easier. "Over at

54

Ashley Packard's lounging around the pool, eating dainty snacks prepared by the maid, visiting with her father's . . . just visiting."

"Who's Ashley Packard?" Dad said. Mom made a somewhat stifled sound.

"This nice girl in my class," I said, "who's going to make me a shoo-in for the St. Joseph Hospital's Junior Board. I'll be modeling in the fashion show next spring. I'm about to turn into a major society babe."

Dad scratched his stubble and tucked in his work shirt. "Well, I guess there's more than one way of going to the dogs."

Which I didn't think was particularly funny.

Chapter Seven

Ashley worked me in. She went on sitting with Lauren Sperling in advisory and sitting by herself in creative writing. But then she usually dealt with everybody one-on-one. She never needed to be in a bunch of girls all screaming and hiding behind each other. She didn't even go to the mall as an addiction. One thing Ashley never did was hang out.

"Besides, I shop with Celia," she said. "It's something we can do together, since we don't have much in common."

That dazzled me. She even worked at being nice to her father's whatever-you-call-it. She worked at being nice to me. When I turned up with a haircut an awful lot like hers, she just approved and wondered who'd done it for me, but she didn't find out. Later toward spring when I did a little something to make it blonder, she very nicely didn't notice.

On the day after Craig Kettering got out of ISS he and Ashley were having lunch together. He was eating pizza and washing it down with the power drink he was still carrying in his personal Thermos. They had one end of a cafeteria table to themselves, with their people giving them space on this first day. Maybe I managed to walk near them with my tray. Ashley waved me over.

I couldn't tell if Craig remembered me, because she said right away, "Here's Chelsea. Come and sit down."

He didn't completely stand up when I joined them, but he came up in a very gentlemanly crouch. You don't get much of that type behavior in a school cafeteria. I hadn't seen the two of them together up close.

Once Ashley had said, "I'm holding Craig in abeyance."

I barely knew the word.

"We're involved, but it's not time to start acting like seniors, let alone like an old married couple. We've both got some growing up to do, especially Craig." We agreed that boys mature more slowly than we do, and Ashley pointed out being a Gremlin as proof.

Craig looked great, in an L. L. Bean–type sweater the other guys would be wanting for Christmas. I remembered that grin featuring the chipped tooth and wondered how he got his sideburns razored that short and neat when no other guy seemed to manage it.

Ashley had brought Craig a present. She was pulling a white T-shirt out of a tote bag and holding it up. The shirt had brown custom lettering across the chest that read,

I AM THE ONLY GREMLIN

"I tried to get it in green and gold, the school colors, you know, but they didn't have—"

Craig grabbed for it over her milk carton and snatched it out of her hand. "Good grief, Ashley, stop waving that thing around."

She giggled somewhat madly.

"You really think you know everything, don't you?" he said. "You think you're a real candidate for the Gifted Program or something." But he was grinning and stuffing the T-shirt under the table.

"Actually, I don't get it," I said, which set them both off again.

"Don't tell Chelsea," he said, grinning proudly.

Ashley turned to me. "It's simple. Craig *was* the only Gremlin. Can you see Spence and Gil and Mark conspiring for weeks on those pranks, without blabbing it all over school? They'd have leaked like sieves."

"They'd also have been in my way while I was getting all that stuff done," Craig added, folding his arms across his chest.

I still didn't get it, quite. "If Craig was on his own in this, how come—"

"They turned themselves in after he got caught by himself. Right, Craig?"

He shrugged, nodded, still grinning. "As soon as they got over the shock of finding out it was me."

"See? I knew it."

"They figured we'd be a great foursome in ISS together," Craig said.

Ashley gave him a long look. "Something like that. They wanted the glory, too, and they can't make a move without their guru. You." She pointed a perfectly manicured finger across the table at him. "We won't even go into why you let yourself get caught. Some people just can't get enough attention."

I guess I thought it was great—having that kind of power over people, having people confess to crimes they didn't even commit just to be where you are. Of course, only guys would do that.

But then Craig started talking about ISS, and it made me kind of nervous, though not nervous enough to leave.

"We called it the zoo because there were some real animals in there and a few mutants. Our keeper was Miss Larrimore."

"What was she like?" I think Ashley was looking at Craig.

"Miss Larrimore? She was all right. Not bad-looking either."

Ashley rolled her eyes heavenward.

"She kept us pretty busy. I probably got more studying done than otherwise. Miss Larrimore's new, so people tried a few things on her, but we settled down after she found somebody's dope."

"Whose?" Ashley asked.

"Just somebody's—not me. Anyway, it was just a roach. One little funny cigarette. She didn't overreact. She just field-stripped it—ran her thumbnail down the cigarette paper, and then it rained expensive grass all over the floor. She ground it in with her heel and said, 'The only benefit from that one went to your dealer.' Then she strolled back to her desk. It had a sobering effect."

60

I was ready to leave then, but now they were talking about something else, something awesome.

"I've already discussed it with Daddy," Ashley was saying, "and he said yes."

"When did your daddy ever say no to you?" Craig said.

"He said yes, but I'm not sure. I'm not sure if we're ready for it."

She was talking about a party for New Year's Eve. The holidays still seemed a ways off to me, but then Ashley was organized. As she often said, the future doesn't solve itself. She was planning a party, a first high-school one, and she was holding it over Craig's head.

"Because I'm not going to end up with all the girls in a bunch on one side of the pool and all the guys on the other, pushing each other into the water and horsing around. If everybody's still going to be junior-high about it, I'm not having a party, period."

But she was going to have the party—"just for a few people," she said. "This is not a class activity."

"Are we going to have dates?" Craig said, "because I could ask Landis Williamson—"

"Not funny, Craig," Ashley said. "And no dating. Just a group of friends. Daddy says we can have wine in moderation, and there'll be real food, not junk. Mabel will see to that. And you'll come, Chelsea."

The bell rang, and I thought the timing was perfect because things couldn't get any better than that.

Over the holidays Mom and I had a head-on collision with each other, at least a fender-bender. I guess we were overdue. For Christmas I'd gotten what I'd campaigned for: real gold and pearl earrings. Pretty expensive, but in good taste. Ashley had a pair a lot like them.

Then I invited Mom to go shopping at Deer Creek Mall. They were having after-Christmas sales anyway. She wasn't as overjoyed at this togetherness as I'd expected her to be.

"I've got to have something to wear to Ashley's party."

We were already in the car, but she'd seen this coming with her radar. Ashley'd said for heaven's sake not to dress up. "This isn't prom night." But of course I had to have something. I didn't have anything.

There was ice in patches on the street from a freak storm, and Mom was concentrating on driving. "You know, we laid out quite a lot for your Christmas present, but now you want something else, something more."

"It's just for this party," I said. "I mean it isn't just for this party. I can wear it a lot. Besides, it's only a sweater. Ashley said we'd wear old jeans and new sweaters. She's keeping it very low-key."

"And how do you feel about being told how to dress?"

"I feel fine about it," I snapped. I wanted to add: *And don't pull your psychological witch-doctoring routine on me.* But I didn't. We were practically in sight of the mall.

"I wonder if I should nip this in the bud," she said. "I wonder if you should."

"I suppose it figures," I said. "You don't want me to be Ashley Packard's friend."

"I know you can't be Ashley Packard."

But that made no sense at all. How could I be Ashley, of all people? For one thing, she didn't even have a mother, not really.

"Look," I said, "we can take the earrings back and exchange them for a sweater." I reached up to my ears, though I wasn't even wearing my Christmas earrings. "Because it's fine with me." I knew I wouldn't have to exchange anything, but I thought it added to my argument. It also meant I wasn't about to settle for some cheap sweater.

Mom didn't say anything, but we got tied up in traffic, and for another long minute the mall didn't get any closer.

"If you knew what the other kids have," I said, "and with credit cards of their own—"

"I know what other kids have," Mom said. "I know kids who don't have anything."

So I wouldn't speak to her again until we were actually in the store itself. I got a sweater I never wore again, and new shoes. I hadn't planned on shoes and didn't particularly like the pair I picked. But I figured Mom had given me some grief, so she owed me.

And on New Year's Eve I thought it was all worth it. The new earrings you had to look twice to see and the new sweater over old jeans which was really low-key. None of us wore any makeup because Ashley didn't need any. Dad put on his old mackinaw jacket and cap and drove me over to the Los Alamitos Country Club Addition.

"Stop here," I said, in front of a dark house.

"But all the lights are on up there." He pointed ahead to the Packards' house.

"I'll get out here," I said. And did.

The house was ablaze with lights and floating in music. The party was in a series of rooms at the back of the courtyard, almost a separate house, with the row of French doors standing open to the pool. There were pinpoint lights in the trees and little candles outlining the shape of the pool. Magic.

Ashley had told me to come early, but lots of people were already there. Maybe she'd told everybody to come early, individually. I wasn't even especially scared, and that felt new and good. My eyes flickered over Landis and Meredith and Dina and Lauren to make sure I looked all right. The guys looked great: Levi's with sport coats in silky weaves pushed up on their arms, really skinny neckties loose at the collar. Except for Craig in an unstructured blazer and a Don Johnson shirt, which he could carry off.

There were adults in the living room in the front part of the house. "We're not chaperons," they kept saying. "We're just here."

When Ashley was introducing me, she ran her arm around her father's middle and said, "It's okay, Daddy. You can be a chaperon if you want to." So of course that kept him away from our party all evening.

She was wearing the perfect thing: an apron. It was long and businesslike, a chef's. It meant she was hostess, in charge but casual. Her new earrings, from Christmas, were diamonds, not flashy, but they caught the light.

64

Her dad, Dr. Packard, was kind of a surprise. Not a hair on his head and not a lot taller than Ashley. Not *as* tall as Celia. He was a little round man smiling and greeting everybody. And Celia hovered behind him in a beautiful dress, a long pillar of glittery stuff.

The man with the pipe standing by the hearth looked familiar. Then the lady sitting in front of the fire looked over her shoulder and said, "Is that son of mine behaving?" She wore a beautiful necklace, and she had Craig's face. So that was Mrs. Kettering, and I saw the man was Craig's stepfather. Nobody lingered long with the adults. We went on to our party.

It was the best night of my life. I kept thinking that. The guys wouldn't dance, but Craig made them mingle. The music was piped out to the courtyard, Laura Branigan singing "Forever Young" over and over. We turned it up so there weren't any awkward silences. Everybody was natural but sort of pumped up. I found the nerve to go to the bathroom with Lauren once, and she just chattered along about Girls' Club like we'd always known each other. I wasn't sure how much the other girls liked me, or how important that was.

Mabel kept bringing out food for the buffet. Bottles of wine stood on a long table. It said BEAUJOLAIS on the label, which I couldn't pronounce, since I wouldn't take French till junior year. I only had a half glass for fear I'd start seeing more lights around the pool than were really there. Some of the guys got loud. Craig got red in the face and finally had to take off his blazer. But then he had Bruce Springsteen arms.

It didn't go on late. We saw the New Year in with some general kissing, mostly on the cheek. Ashley'd

65

said we didn't have to stay up all night just to prove we were past puberty, so I told Dad to come back for me at one-thirty. When I came out of the Packards' house, he was sitting in the Dodge, three doors down.

I thought it'd be a straight shot from that night to the Junior Board fashion show and turning sixteen and getting our licenses. I looked ahead at the new year, and it seemed to have wings. I'd come farther than I'd ever expected to. Overlooking the fact that Mom's job had brought us here, I thought it was a miracle we'd moved to this place and these people.

I'll tell you what I thought: that all my life I'd been watching on a black-and-white set. And now I had a small part in the production, and it was in full color.

Chapter Eight

The new year was slower than I'd hoped, winding down toward the end of the semester. But Pod was never far off. Every once in a while in the cafeteria I'd hear this voice up against my ear, saying, "Care to have me for lunch?"

Otherwise he'd feed at the trough (his own phrase) over at a table of fairly dorky tenth-grade boys. At the trough he gripped his fork like a bike handle and called everybody "stud hoss." Occasionally he'd have lunch with Ruth Baines, which I thought was nice of him.

In creative writing he was over his Nashville sound and at work on his "novel." It was about a character named V. C. Clanton who was too macho for Rambo. In Pod's own words, V.C. was the King of the Cow-chip Kickers. He ate silage for breakfast and drove a road grader on dates. When he went to tractor pulls, he pulled against the tractor and won. When he went to barn dances, he danced with the barn.

Class criticism of Pod's novel ranged from "over-written" to "totally gross." But all Mr. Mallory said was that "Pod echoes Paul Bunyan's essentially American quest for manliness in the midst of a matriarchy."

Pod looked pleased. He stretched his saga to come out even with the end of the semester when V.C. met the woman of his dreams and they rode off into the sunset. Her name was Shirley Dew Hopeso.

It didn't dawn on me till later that Mr. Mallory had been our hardest teacher and we never knew it. He invited us to put ourselves on the line, to take some steps away from who we were and to take some chances on those blank pages. I didn't come up with much. I was too busy protecting myself to create anything. Pod was self-protective too: building his image and then playing it for laughs. I couldn't have done that much. And of course I couldn't write the kind of poetry Ashley read.

Her poems didn't flow out of her, which I thought showed what it cost her to write them. She'd give us time to look forward to them, and we did. I did. Every poem was a layer she peeled back to show she was vulnerable too. I thought if I hadn't been in creative writing with her, I wouldn't have known her at all.

Then on the last day of the semester she read the last poem.

"There isn't usually a title—I don't usually title them," she said. "But this one's called 'Girl in the Mirror.'"

68

It was the only one of the poems that rhymed, and she faltered in a couple of places as she read.

> *Her lips move when mine do.*
> *'I'll show you me if you'll show me you.'*
>
> *I see her in the mornings when we compare faces,*
> *I pass her in windows, unexpected places.*
>
> *I'd like to read her mind and look her in the eye,*
> *I'd like to know her better, but I'm shy.*
>
> *'Who are you?'*
> *Shall I form the question,*
> *Give it to her?*
>
> *Or shall I take the easy way*
> *And merely look right through her?*

Somehow that poem gave all her others a shape. It was the perfect last one, maybe because it ended with a question. I liked it that Ashley, who seemed to have all the answers, still had questions.

We were quiet when she finished. It was a moody, gray day, and we were heading into finals. Mr. Mallory was at his desk, pulling on his long chin. Unexpectedly, he said, "What do you think, Pod?"

His cap was on the back of his head, and he was looking down, running a ballpoint over the graffiti on his desk. He shrugged, and then looked up at Ashley. "It's a good poem," he said without his drawl. "The rhythm's off, and that's okay because the girl in the poem's uncertain too." He hadn't taken his eyes off Ashley. "I liked it as soon as I heard it."

She glanced away, and somebody said, "Ashley

ought to get her poetry together and send it in to a contest or something." A lot of people nodded. I nodded.

Ashley shook her head. "I don't think so." Then, maybe because she remembered this was the last day of the class, she said, "Later when I have time to work them over, I might do something with them." She brightened and quoted Mr. Mallory's favorite saying. " 'The only good writing is rewriting.' " Her elbows were planted on her desktop over the poem page, and her face was cupped in her hands. It looked wise in the way a fox's mask does.

And that was the end of creative writing class. For a second-semester elective I took fashion merchandising even though Ashley'd already taken it first semester. For my other elective I managed to get into drivers' ed. I dropped chorus because nobody was in it.

I was clinging to the bottom of the Honor Roll with three B's and an A in my majors. Ashley got all C's except for a D and the A she got in creative writing. I couldn't believe it. At Crestwood they save C's for the airheads, and you only get a D for deciding not to try.

"But then I'm not particularly bright," she said when we got our grades. That wasn't even true. I couldn't figure it out.

"Won't your folks—"

"Daddy won't mind, and Mother won't know, and Celia doesn't count." She smiled and shook her head in a way that meant she was way ahead of all of them. Then she brushed her locker door shut, and off we all went to Registration.

At least she got an A from Mr. Mallory. We all did,

and we fell for it. Afterward it dawned on me that giving everybody an A might have been his ironic statement about us, maybe our whole school system. He liked irony. He was English.

And still the year didn't develop wings. At that age you waste a lot of time waiting for something wonderful to happen. The winter was weird, too, skittish. There'd be seventy-degree days, and then everything skimmed with ice. Spring came earlier than I expected. It was spring in February and summer almost in March.

By then I'd copied as much as I could from Ashley and the others. I was trying for something more—something in the air around them that I wanted around me. It gave me something to think about when Ashley wasn't around. I knew not to try to take up more of her time than she had to give me. Pod noticed my changes because there's nothing wrong with his beady eyesight.

Then one day he tried to spoil everything, one mean March day.

By then I thought I was walking like Meredith, who dances and has great posture. I had a little gesture from Lauren. I forget what I'd borrowed from Dina, but from Landis, who was the most beautiful, I was hoping for some self-confidence. And at least I had earrings and hair like Ashley. Her birthday was first, which was logical, and so I was thinking about her birthday party coming up. It was to be a production, and the invitations were out, and I had one.

Then Pod came past my locker one day after school. I thought: Here I am with all these great traits, so I should try them out on him. I turned with Meredith's posture and scooped the hair back from my forehead in

71

Lauren's way. Just as confident as Landis, I started to say, *Hi, Pod,* and then I went for Ashley's smile, the crinkly one with lights.

He had on his old denim jacket with the FFA patch and the plaid cap with the flaps he'd worn all winter. Instead of staggering backward from all my borrowed brilliance, he just stopped. "Chelsea?" No drawl. No twang.

He wasn't even in a hurry suddenly, and after school he usually was. He rode the school bus and didn't like being seen climbing onto it. But his birthday wasn't till summer, so he couldn't have driven in from the country every day even if he had a car. So usually he cut out fast. But not today.

"Walk me out to the bus?" he said, which I'd never done.

I looked past his shoulder as if Ashley might be there and we'd have plans. But she wasn't there, and we didn't have plans. So I gave him another one of her smiles that just dawned on me. I guess Pod saw whose smile it was, so I'll never know if he'd been planning to tell me what he told me.

When we got out to the buses, I said, "What are we doing out here? Is this a date?" That gave him an opening for one of his punch lines, but he didn't take it. Country kids were milling around us. Pod stood with both hands in his back pockets. He looked like he wished I wasn't there, or he hadn't asked me.

"Why don't you just ease off on Ashley?"

"What are you talking about?"

"Something that's none of my business." He

squinted across the parking lot, where junior and senior cars were peeling out.

"As long as you know," I said.

"You don't need her."

"I don't need anybody," I said to him. "Think about
it."

"I'm not trying to make you mad," he said. "It'd be
easier just to climb up on the old bus, you know."

So go, I nearly said, but didn't. "You're like my
mother. She's scared to death I'll have friends, probably because she never had any."

Pod looked at me, through me. "You ought to watch
your step with Ashley. She'll let you down. Be ready."

He really had my attention, so I just looked away. "Is
that it?" I said. "You want to catch your bus now?"

"I've got another couple of minutes," he said.

"Pod, you don't know a couple of minutes' worth
about Ashley. I know her quite a bit better than you
ever will."

"Do you know where her poetry came from? All that
good stuff she read in Mallory's class?"

The wind came up, blowing dirt. People turned their
faces away from it. I did.

"It's Ruth Baines's poetry. She wrote it in ninth
grade. Ruth wrote a lot of poetry, reams of it."

"How do you know—"

"I know Ruth. She's kind of an introvert. She is an
introvert. I'm not. I'd talk to her. She showed me her
stuff. It's her poetry, about her."

I remembered how I'd waited to hear Ashley read
her poetry, whenever she . . . had one to read.

"Ashley doesn't even know Ruth Baines," I said.

73

"Why should she? And what are you saying, that she stole the poetry?"

Pod shook his head. "She bought it. Five bucks a poem."

His bus stood there, and the driver hadn't even started honking yet. Nothing moved. And I believed him, so I betrayed Ashley.

"Ruth Baines must be a crazy person," I said.

"And yet you liked what you knew of her in those poems."

"That was when— Anyhow, you've got to be wrong. Why would Ruth sell her poems anyway?"

Pod turned up his hands. "If Ruth had read those poems in a class, which she wouldn't have, nobody'd have cared or even listened. We've all been together since grade school, so Ruth's been watching Ashley wing it and use people for years. I guess Ruth just figured she'd make her pay for once. It worked out for both of them. Which is fine, as long as nobody else gets fooled. I don't think Mallory was. I think he smelled a rat."

The driver tapped the bus horn a little late. "You gonna hate me forever?" Pod hunched up in his jacket.

"Maybe not forever," I said, "but for now."

He had one boot up on the step of the bus, but I seemed to need another last word. "So what am I supposed to do, go and make friends with Ruth Baines?"

"You could do worse," Pod said over his shoulder. "In fact—"

But I turned around and walked away.

I wasn't about to make friends with Ruth Baines. Why should I? And I didn't want to know that Ashley's

74

poetry was actually hers. Still, I managed to run into Ruth the next day. I was cutting through the gym at noon, and she was sitting down low in the bleachers, eating a sandwich and writing something in a notebook. I could have breezed past her, but didn't.

When she saw me sort of hovering, she looked up and gave a little half smile. "Hi, Chelsea."

She closed her notebook but kept her place in it with her thumb. I knew how that felt. I hate people looking at my private stuff. And I didn't want to see hers, especially if it was poetry.

"How's it going?" I said, inspired.

"All right." She brought her shoulders up a little. Why did she dress like that—like she was trying not to be there? I wanted to ask her things I didn't want answers for.

She slipped her thumb out of her notebook and pushed it down the polished bleacher. "I can't take the din in that cafeteria every day," she said, and reached into a brown bag to pull out an apple, a polished red delicious.

She held it out to me. An offering. I took it for something to do, wondering where the conversation was going to come from. With Ashley you don't need to worry. She takes the lead and keeps it. She speaks her lines and yours too. I edged onto the end of the bleacher but kept one foot on the floor. "You like to write," I said.

The glare of the gym lights on her glasses nearly hid her eyes, but she was in there. "I need another world to be in some of the time." She glanced around at the big cavern of the gym, but she could be lonely anywhere.

75

In a way, so can I.

"When you're writing," Ruth said, "you're talking to somebody who listens."

That made sense too. Even the writing I'd done in Mallory's class had made me feel that way. In real life you're never that sure anybody's really listening. Except maybe for Pod, who hears too much.

"Did you . . ." I started to ask her about Ashley, but tapered off—wimped out.

"What?" She looked right at me. We were communicating almost too well for words.

"Nothing."

But she knew what I'd decided not to ask. I know because she said, "I'm leaving Crestwood after this year. My parents want me to go to private school. It's a stretch for them financially, but they say the classes will be smaller."

I guess her parents thought she might be less lonely in a smaller place. She smiled at that, as if she couldn't be a loner anywhere.

Later, long after she was gone, I thought of Ruth as a lost opportunity, a chance for somebody I could really talk to. But at the time I wasn't ready for that. At the time I was just relieved she'd be leaving school, going someplace where you didn't have to think about her. Besides, I didn't want any of her loneliness rubbing off on me.

Chapter Nine

Ashley's sixteenth birthday party was going to be the best. People—Dina and Meredith and Lauren and even self-confident Landis—said they weren't going to try to compete when their birthdays came. It was only to be for a few girls, the usual few.

"No boys," Ashley said, "so we can just be ourselves, and it's definitely not going to be their kind of thing."

She was having a "Color Me Lovely" party, which was put on by this lady in town who's a professional about makeup and clothes coordination. She comes to your house for a girls' party and charges seventy dollars a guest to give tips, and you get a "cosmetic consultation" and free samples.

Basically it was to be a hoot because Ashley didn't even wear makeup and sure didn't need advice about coordinating her wardrobe. Which I suppose was the point. But she said it'd be fun, and it would get the two of us ready for the St. Joseph's Junior Board fashion show, and besides, Celia was thrilled.

"Don't buy me presents," Ashley told everybody. "We'll get all those free samples, and I don't need anything anyway."

But I decided to give Ashley a present, a free one she wouldn't even know about. For her birthday I was going to forget what Pod had told me about her. I was going to forget it so much that it never happened.

We decorated her locker on her birthday, like a parade float. And her party went just the way she said it would because that's how things worked for her. It started with a surprise: she was out of her braces. We didn't notice at first because she smiled small, but then we all screamed when we saw, though we weren't screamers.

Mabel's food was terrific. The Color Me Lovely lady was all right, except she was too serious about her work and not serious enough about us. She treated us like we were at a sixteenth birthday party instead of being a lot older, which is what we wanted to be. And Celia hovered too much, in the doorway, where she was trying to take part in the party without intruding.

After the cosmetics lady had gone, leaving the place littered with samples of gloss and mousse and cucumber cold cream, Ashley slipped away to her bathroom. She came back with all the Color Me Lovely makeup scrubbed off her face and her hair tucked casually back behind her ears. So we gave her a round of applause. We all went and scrubbed our faces, too, which meant we were above this sort of thing. Celia looked confused

78

and a little troubled, and Ashley didn't mind that either.

Then Dr. Packard came up to the French doors and looked into the party room with owlish bifocals. "I see this is a hen party, so I'll just have Celia deliver this to the birthday girl." He was holding out a little black velvet box for Celia to take.

But she said, "Oh, no, honey, you give it to her." Celia held back, so Dr. Packard padded across the room in bedroom slippers to Ashley.

She was on the floor in the circle of us with her legs tucked neatly under her. She looked up at her father in surprise, and she wasn't surprised. He bent down, bowing, and opened his hand to give her the little box. "For my princess," he said, as if they were the only two in the room or the world.

In the quietness she opened the box. "Oh, Daddy," she said softly, and held up the keys to a car.

It was a little robin's-egg-blue Mustang convertible with white top and upholstery and wire wheels. We all flew out of the house and around the pool to where it was parked in front of the garages. There was a huge white bow across the hood, and we stood around it while Ashley slipped behind the wheel. The moon was out that night, part of some master plan, beaming white light down on Ashley behind the wheel of her car, at the controls. Celia stood in the shadows, watching.

Though I'd cooled off a lot on Pod, I told him all about the party. I guess I described it to let him know

79

that nothing he'd said about Ashley meant anything to me. Anyhow, it'd been a perfect party, from the beginning without the braces, to the end with the car, and I wanted to talk about it. He listened and didn't say anything, which I thought was sulky of him, sullen.

There weren't many more landmarks in the long spring semester, though when Craig's birthday came, he got a 450 SL, claret-red. I wasn't slated for a car of my own, but I was learning to drive in drivers' ed. I'd even gotten through the gross part: that film they show you called *Mechanized Death*. Somebody threw up on a desk after the first three minutes of it, but it wasn't me.

Then the weather turned hot, and it was almost time for finals and summer. It was the last week of classes, and I wasn't thinking about much but the rehearsals coming up for the Junior Board fashion show. I'd wanted to do a little informal rehearsing with Ashley, but she didn't mention it, or need it. So I practiced by myself, walking up and down in my room, trying to turn it into a long runway and myself into a model. I wasn't too nervous, because I couldn't even believe it would happen. And as a matter of fact, it never did.

On the afternoon of our last biology lab, we began to hear sirens outside, a noise from another world breaking through. I didn't really know anybody in biology and didn't have much to say to my lab partner, Jimmy Delgado. We'd been dissecting pigs, but we'd finally gotten through the intestinal tract, which had been one long mess. When we heard the sirens in the school drive, Jimmy said, "Paramedics."

Nobody went to the windows. We didn't do that in Mr. Gruener's lab. Then there was another wave of sound, another siren. Police, according to Jimmy. We heard them outside, hitting their brakes. People were running in the halls, heavy-footed, clanking like cops.

When Mr. Gruener spoke, he was just turning back from the window that looks down on the drive. "Chelsea, go to the office."

People looked up from their pigs, back at me. I went, in a dream. There were still voices out in the hall, but I didn't see anything. I never quite made it to the office. Mr. Hodge, a guidance counselor, was just coming back in the front doors, running. "Chelsea!" I didn't know he knew me.

He gripped my shoulder and held me for a moment like he didn't know which direction to send me in. First he looked down the row of offices, and then back over his shoulder, outdoors. Then he ran with me through the front door, out into blinding sunshine. Two cop cruisers were pulling away, but the paramedic van was there. I knew before I knew.

By the open van doors there was a cot on wheels, and they were just ready to lift it inside. I slipped away from Mr. Hodge. The figure on the cot was wrapped tight in a blanket. There was a towel, too, soaked red. I went closer to see. It was Mom. It was my mother, gray in the blazing day with half her face hidden by the towel. They rolled her into the van. They were taking away Miss Larrimore.

Chapter Ten

Finals were the next week, and I took them. But this was final enough for me. The day Mom went to the hospital was the real end of sophomore year.

That evening Dad and I sat outside Intensive Care, waiting between the times a doctor or intern or somebody came out to say something. I sat there, wanting the voices out of my head. Mom's voice. Ages ago in August she'd said, "You'll just feel silly when they find out."

I hadn't wanted anybody to know that Miss Larrimore, the new guidance counselor in ISS, was my mother. For work she used her maiden name because it was an up-to-date thing to do and because I didn't want anyone linking us up. I had enough of her at home. I didn't want teachers expecting anything special out of me. I didn't want people pointing me out. Mom's job was to look into the lives of teenagers, and I didn't want her looking into mine. I had these reasons.

Whenever we'd met in the hallways at school, I just looked the other way. It seemed to work. Now I sat next to Dad in this green corridor, not knowing whether . . . Nurses went by on squeaky shoes. People rolled past on carts. No glamor here, no *General Hospital,* and smells you didn't need.

I hadn't wanted anybody to know. Now I was forgetting why exactly. People knew. Teachers knew and hadn't mentioned it. Mr. Gruener in biology, the most impersonal, buttoned-down human being in school, knew. He'd looked out the window to see Mom down by the van and turned directly to me. Mom went to faculty meetings with these people. They had this relationship going. Adults had their groups too. Could this just be dawning on me? Ashley knew. Somehow I was sure Ashley'd known all along.

The school kept everything out of the newspapers. But people knew what had happened to Mom because there were plenty of witnesses when this girl in ISS named Gloria Raymond attacked her.

I didn't know Gloria Raymond. She wasn't around much, and I wouldn't have known her anyway. Nobody knew whether she was a junior or what. I never did see her, but I had a picture of her in my mind. One of those girls with an inch of makeup over pasty skin, too much hair, purple nails, a little flabby from junk food. She'd be the kind you see after school, lighting up and climbing on the back of some sweat's bike.

One day she turned up at school, stoned from the night before. They stuck her in ISS. And without a word Gloria Raymond just walked up the aisle to Mom's desk, picked up a metal wastebasket, and swung it against the side of Mom's face.

"Concussion," one of the doctor/interns came out to say, "and stitches over the cheekbone, of course. But she's looking lucky about the eye. May be a longer-term problem with peripheral vision, but that's later."

I don't know if Dad heard. I don't know what he'd heard after he found out it was a girl who'd attacked Mom. It left him more helpless.

The doctor told us to go home because she'd sleep through the night. That had been an hour ago, and Dad hadn't moved. Nobody was around now, nobody we knew. It was like the first day in a new town. Dad sat forward on the bench, hunched.

I saw what I was waiting for. I was waiting for him to make it all right, to be in charge. I was giving him time.

Then he said, "This isn't the way it's supposed to be. I'm lost."

He worked his hands over his knees. His big shoulders were slumped, unsteady. He wasn't being strong enough, not nearly. He wasn't being my dad, and I felt myself pulling away. "Don't," he said. "Not you too."

"We ought to go home," I said. "They told us to."

He checked the wall clock again and ran his hand through his hair where it was thin. The skull tattoo on his arm moved in the air.

"I ought to feed the pups," he said. "They'll raise the neighborhood." He sat up straighter but didn't move. He couldn't leave Mom unless I helped him.

"You go. I'll stay here. And don't forget Lucy, wherever she is. She goes up in my room when we aren't home, and she knows she's not supposed to, so she hides. Go take care of them and then come back." I thought when he came back I could get him home again. "You go," I said, trying to sound like Mom.

He wasn't gone long. I almost dozed off, but I was afraid I'd dream, and then he was back. I didn't let him sit down or anything. I got him back outside.

In the truck he said, "Can you drive good enough to follow me home?" Because Mom's Dodge was still in the school parking lot. I'd blocked that out with the rest of school.

"The pups had been fed," he said as we pulled away from the hospital. "Not Lucy. She was up in your closet, trying to sit on your shoes. But the pups were fed—overfed. Fresh water too. A kid was there, doing it."

"Who?"

"Johnson? Pod Johnson? I didn't know what to say. I didn't know who he was." We were on the big street that loops around the city, with car dealerships on it. "The kid said he was a friend of yours. He thought he'd stop by and see if there was anything he could do. I hope I thanked him."

The Dodge was standing alone in the school parking lot. Dad pulled up, and the extra set of keys was in his hand.

"We came here for her job," he said. "It looked good. It looked like an opportunity for her. What did I know? When I went to school, I can tell you, a teacher was safe—more than that. Why did I let this happen? If I'd had a real job and done better, she wouldn't have had to—"

"No." I had to fill up the cab with words. "Mom would want a job anyway, a career. She's ambitious and organized and always looking ahead. She wouldn't want to sit home." How did I know this? "Women don't want to stay home. This isn't . . . the past."

I wasn't sure this was me explaining these things. Not after a year of trying to pretend Mom and her job didn't even exist. I wasn't ready for this, and did he even hear me? He was staring out at the lonely Dodge parked neatly in the empty lot.

Then he made a fist against the rim of the steering wheel and leaned forward to rest his forehead on it. "Wait," he said, and I waited while he fought with himself. In a little while he dropped the keys in my hand, and I followed him in Mom's Dodge, keeping the right distance.

He'd left lights on at home, but it was like coming back after years. I was almost too tired to see. I wanted him to take over and make everything right, and it was too late for that.

He was locking up when I remembered and turned back from the stairs. "You're okay? You won't go out again?" I had to ask. I was the only one here to ask.

"Where would I go?"

I made myself say it. "Out for a drink."

He looked at me, surprised. "Has that been bothering you? Chelsea, drink isn't the problem."

I'd have let it go at that, gladly, but he wasn't finished.

"Sometimes I think your mom married me because she's good at dealing with . . . hard cases. I try not to be a lost cause for her."

He didn't say anything more, just rubbed his hand over his mouth. I went on upstairs because nothing was the way it was supposed to be. Crazy Lucy was out of my closet and sprawled all over the stairs. I fell over her where she was trying to lie on two steps with her paws stuck out a mile. But I went on. When I got to my room, I thought about crying, but I was too tired.

They moved Mom to a room, and we sat with her through the next day, spelling one another. She was awake but bleary. She didn't want her breakfast or her lunch. One side of her face was so swollen she didn't like to talk. A track of black stitches made an ugly shape over her swollen cheek. The white of her eye was flooded with red. She was someone else, who I was visiting in a hospital scene that didn't relate to anything. I poured a lot of water for her.

Dad and I were both there over lunchtime. He'd done a funny thing—brought in a puppy hidden in his jacket, and a nipple bottle of milk because it wasn't quite weaned. People were beginning to dump dogs on him, use him instead of the pound. This one was the runt of a litter, and he was supposed to put it to sleep, but instead he was looking for a good home for it. It looked like the product of two breeds that shouldn't be crossed.

He put it on the bed, where it started rolling around. I guess he'd brought it as a distraction. I kept a distance from the dogs we deal with. When I was a lot younger, a puppy had died in my hands. It was there, and then it was gone.

Mom wasn't too interested in this little fur ball climbing her sheets either. But then she looked at me, remembering. "School?" she said, slurred out of the corner of her mouth, but I shook my head. I wasn't going. Not today, not tomorrow.

After Dad left, the phone by her bed rang, and it was the school secretary to say how concerned they all were. I don't know what I said. When I hung up, Mom was looking at the phone, her head turned so she could see it with her good eye. We didn't get company till the second day.

Mom was better that morning. The swelling was down, but the bruising was darker, spread down her neck into the loose hospital gown. A woman came in, and Mom saw her first. She had on a plasticky car coat and jeans, and her bleached hair stood out around her face.

"You Miss Larrimore?" She looked away, then back.

Mom stirred in the bed; pulled the sheet tighter.

"I'm Lois Raymond," the woman said, "Gloria's mother. They told me not to come, but I thought I would."

"Who told you?" Mom's voice was hardly slurred.

The woman fiddled with the catch on her purse. "Oh, you know, everybody." She fiddled some more, digging her hand in the purse. "Can you smoke in here?"

But Mom only looked at her.

"I've tried to raise her, but you know how kids are." She didn't seem to see me there, but then she probably didn't think Miss Larrimore had any kids. I suppose she was the only one I ever fooled.

89

"Yes, I know how kids are," Mom said.

"Well, you don't know Gloria," the woman said, sighing. "You wouldn't have had the chance to get to know her. I have a job, so I haven't been able to ride herd on her like she probably needed."

"I have a job too," Mom said.

"She was out of that house at the age of twelve like greased lightning." The woman—Mrs. Raymond—looked at the end of Mom's bed and thought about parking her purse there. "And she's boy-crazy. She developed early like I did. And I couldn't do a thing in this world with her. I told her she was heading for trouble, and she laughed in my face."

"She did worse than that to me," Mom said.

The woman looked aside. "I blame the school, really," she said. "When Gloria was in junior high, they'd call me at work if she was cutting. But they're lax about that in high school, so how am I supposed to know where she is or what's happening?"

"I can assure you she was in school yesterday." It was Mom's voice, but the words didn't sound like her. "And I hope she's in jail today."

"Well, no," Mrs. Raymond said. "They called me from the station last night and scared the daylights out of me. I'd just gotten home from work and had to turn around and go down there, as if I didn't have enough to do. I told them she was seventeen, and they released her in my custody."

"How old is she?"

"She's eighteen, the youngest of three—the baby. I don't know where she is now. She wouldn't come home with me."

90

"Your daughter needs psychiatric care," Mom said.

Mrs. Raymond had trouble looking Mom in the face, but she looked now. "Well, no," she said, "we've never had anything like that in the family."

"Your daughter needs psychiatric care. She's violent. She's desperate. She probably has a chemical addiction. She needs family counseling that will involve you."

"I do the best I—"

"She should have been in a special school for disturbed children, a controlled environment. We have a school like that in this system."

"Nobody ever told me about it. Gloria probably wouldn't have wanted to go to it, but I had a right to know. They don't tell you a thing. They call you in for these conferences and when you don't show up, they just let it go. Of course, it's too late now. I don't think Gloria will be coming back to school. I'm not going to encourage it."

"Is that what you came here to tell me?" Mom said.

Mrs. Raymond's eyes snapped. "I came to tell you I'm sorry. I don't know if I should have." She turned to go, digging for her cigarettes. When Mom didn't say any more, she turned back at the door. "I just don't want any trouble, is all I mean." Then she was gone.

After a moment Mom said, "I think that wore me out."

"What did it mean?"

"Just what she said. She doesn't want any trouble. She doesn't want me trying to press charges against her, or the school bothering her."

"Will you? Will they?"

91

"No."

"But why?"

"The school won't want any publicity, because it's bad public relations. And I haven't any leverage as a first-year teacher acting on my own. I even have a case against the school for not providing me with any kind of safety, but I'll be lucky to get compensation out of them for this hospital bill. I've been on this job a year. I know how things work. The school will just suggest to Mrs. Raymond that Gloria shouldn't return, which is what she wants to hear anyway."

I didn't understand it, or want to. This didn't even sound like the same school I went to every day. It was too confusing and not fair.

"Why did Gloria Raymond do that to you?"

Mom looked toward the window, and I saw the side of her face I knew.

"Why? I guess she was just—overcome with anger at the whole adult world for letting her be what she is. And she knew she'd get away with it. She's scared too. It's scary when you know you won't be held responsible, for anything. Your whole generation seems to be having that problem."

I didn't know what that meant, either, and didn't particularly like being lumped in with Gloria Raymond. There are plenty of Gloria Raymonds out there, and they didn't have anything to do with me.

Anyway, it was Mom's problem. She was sounding good today, almost her old self with even extra spunk. I'd have put all our old distance between us again, except we had another visitor that afternoon, after school. Ashley came.

Chapter Eleven

The flowers she sent came first. It was a big summer arrangement with painted daisies and birds of paradise. Mom was dozing when Ashley came into the room. She stood inside the door, straight from school, but she looked like she'd just come from changing her clothes. I hadn't thought about what I was wearing for days. She was just like she always was, and I was ready to get back to that.

She glanced at Mom and away. It meant we were supposed to go outside where we could talk. There was a room where you could sit at the end of a hall.

"You knew who my mom was," I said. She hadn't said anything to anybody about it, which I thought was great.

"I was just waiting for you to get around to telling," she said. "It was your story to tell. Everybody knows now, so it doesn't matter. Even Craig's figured out who

Miss Larrimore in ISS was. You know boys. They take their time."

I saw she'd been . . . discreet. It seemed to me she was better than adults, more mature. We talked a little about what had happened, and her voice was low, concerned. She hadn't known who Gloria Raymond was. Why would she? Nothing like that could come close to Ashley's life. And yet as we sat together on the wheezing plastic sofa, her eyes said she understood.

But she was looking at her watch. Then she was on her feet, busy and committed as always, too quick for me to move.

"And listen," she said, half turned away, "don't worry about that Junior Board fashion show business. The rehearsals and fittings are this week, and I know you can't be bothered with all that now. I've asked Dina to fill in for you, and she said yes. Some of the clothes are in petite sizes, so she'll be fine."

I couldn't speak. I couldn't have heard her right. She was ready to walk, but looked back.

"It's all right, isn't it? We didn't know what to think about your mother's condition. It's great that she's doing so well, but we didn't know. I did the right thing, didn't I?"

So I had to say yes, at least nod. Then she was gone, saying she'd call, saying she'd see me or something. And still I didn't know what had happened.

I was on my feet, staring down at the polished floor because Ashley had just pulled the rug out from under me. But I didn't have time to figure it out. I had to get back to Mom, right away. When I burst back into her room, she was awake, sitting up.

"You're not going to die, are you?"

She couldn't do anything with one side of her face, but the other half looked quite surprised. "Eventually," she said, "not anytime soon."

"Are you going to quit your job?" I didn't know what answer I wanted from that.

"Don't you believe it," she said. "I've got a career plan. Haven't I told you?"

Probably, and I hadn't heard.

"I want Miss Wilmot's job when she retires next year. I want to be a college counselor. Haven't you noticed me lugging around those college catalogs all the time?"

Maybe.

"They told me I had to take ISS before I was in line for the other job. Now I mean to have it. They owe me."

"Oh," I murmured.

She looked at me as closely as she could.

"I'm not going to get any justice out of this, you know. I'm not going to get Gloria Raymond separated from society, and I'm not going to be able to sue her awful mother, because she's probably more broke than we are. And look around you in this room. Do you see anybody here? Do you see me getting any backup from my colleagues?"

I couldn't help it. I looked around the room.

"Let me tell you what they're thinking," she said. "The faculty at that school aren't here because suddenly I'm a victim, and that makes them more vulnerable. And where are the administrators? They've dealt with me by a call from the principal's secretary."

Her good eye was practically sending out sparks, and the reddish lights in her hair were practically strobing. I've mentioned her temper. It was really pretty impressive.

"So then," I said carefully, "why don't you—"

"Because I need this job," she said. "And because I'm going to make this work for me. That school's full of kids drifting because nobody's in charge of their lives. That school needs me. Believe it."

I did. I did.

I saw Mom then, maybe for the first time. There she was, battered bad by a kid because she was trying to do something for kids whose own parents can't and don't care. I saw her there in the bed, beat up and planning.

She settled back and almost smiled with half a mouth. "Now that everybody knows who I am and who you are, can you live with the shame?"

I couldn't quite say I'd be proud, so I stood at the foot of her bed trying to look proud.

"And by the way," she said, "you look like somebody's just dealt you a nasty blow too. Was it Ashley?"

So there Mom went again, reading my mind. I still didn't like it. It was witchy.

❦

Ashley wrote twice over the summer, a pair of postcards, and the first one was from Paris.

She'd gone to Europe right after the fashion show, with Dina Westervelt and her family. Dina's father was with some government fact-finding commission. On the postcard of the Louvre Ashley wrote only a couple of lines, but I could read between them. She'd had a chance to tour Europe on the embassy level with the very political Westervelt family, and that's why Dina got to be in the fashion show instead of me.

They'd worked a trade-off: Europe for Ashley and the fashion show for Dina, gnomish Dina. Even I could figure that out. How dumb was I supposed to be? The newspaper picture that had run about the fashion show was of Ashley coming down the runway in the Grand Ballroom of the Hyatt Hotel. The outfit she was modeling, in June, was a back-to-school number, and that was just right because Ashley always looks ahead.

Junior Year

Chapter Twelve

Ashley's second card came in August, from L.A., where she'd gone on to visit her mother. It was a Disneyland card, meant as a hoot, and she wrote in the voice of a Valley girl, her commentary on California: *The guys out here are like fine wine, hang ten and luv ya forever, Ashley.*

But by August other things had happened. The world doesn't stop when Ashley's away, quite. In the week Mom got her stitches out, long after she was home again, I had my sixteenth birthday. Dad took me down to the Motor Vehicle office at Deer Creek Mall, and I showed them my driving skill, and they gave me a license.

I went looking for a job because I could use some money, and I didn't want to hang around home working for Dad and being too near Mom. We'd taken a half step closer to each other, but I didn't want to push my luck.

The only job I could find was at a Sizzler. They assigned me to the salad bar, which will keep me from being a vegetarian for life. I spent the summer trying to keep the pickled beets from bleeding into the corn relish.

But it was all right. I figured nobody would see me there, wearing that ridiculous uniform and cap. None of Ashley's people ever came in there anyway, or Craig's.

A funny thing happened because of my Sizzler job. I came home in the Dodge one afternoon between shifts, and a street rod was parked right in front of the kennels, a 1940 Mercury ragtop. The ground was littered with tools, and two pairs of legs stuck out from under the car. I knew Dad's legs right away; you can't miss them. There was something familiar about the other pair too: bowlegged with Levi's riding low. Then Dad rolled out from under the car, and so did—Pod.

It seemed that Pod was now working for Dad, at four and a quarter an hour. Since I was at Sizzler, which Pod knew because he'd called up exactly once and we talked, he figured Dad needed some help around the kennels. The fact that they spent most of Pod's working hours under the rod didn't seem to be a major concern.

I stood there, absorbing this new turn of events. I wasn't in a great mood anyway. In my Sizzler uniform I never was.

"That's all I need, Pod. We're together all year long at school, and now you'll be here every time I come home. I'll tell you the truth. If I was picking brothers, you wouldn't be my first choice, no offense meant."

And none taken apparently. Pod had enough axle

102

grease on his face to infiltrate enemy lines. For summer wear he'd given up a cap in favor of a red bandana rolled into a tube around his forehead: Rambo-before-puberty. He was grinning big.

"But wait till you see this sweetheart when I get it in shape." He patted the bulging Mercury fender. "Wait till you see twenty-three coats of enamel on her—maroon. Under the hood she's already sweet as cream. And look, running boards." He pointed out one with his boot toe.

What are you going to do? For the rest of the summer I'd get home to find Pod and Dad either coming back with guns and dogs from up in the hills, or they'd be under the Mercury. Dad sometimes hummed a song called "Little Deuce Coupe" from the Beach Boys. And Pod turned into this authority on dogs. Such phrases as *olfactory prowess* and *nose-worthiness* flowed from his lips.

I didn't like it much. I'd always wanted Dad to myself, even when I wasn't around. In an indirect way I even complained to Mom, but she just mentioned something about "male bonding" which I didn't follow.

Then the summer slipped away, and we were on the verge of school again, junior year. And Ashley came back. There was a knock at the door, and out the window I saw her robin's-egg-blue convertible, standing there like an ad. Ashley was on the other side of the door, and I didn't want to see her, and I couldn't wait. At least I didn't have my Sizzler uniform on, because that job was over for the season. I glanced around the room to see if things were picked up. Then, looking surprised, I opened the door.

She stood there California-tanned and Paris-topped in a Ton sur Ton jacket with push-up sleeves and many pockets. It was going to be a very big look at Crestwood that year. She looked a pound or two thinner, an inch or two taller, worldly.

She put out her arms, and I tried not to fall into them. But we hugged and allowed ourselves a squeal or two. Suddenly things were going to be better than ever. She was into the room, and her eyes went everywhere—to the stairs. Mom was standing there.

"Hello, Miss—Mrs. Olinger." Ashley's smile bathed the room in golden light.

"I would have written to thank you for the beautiful flowers," Mom said, "but you left so soon, for Europe."

I flashed her a warning look, because she didn't have any right to . . . say anything to Ashley about dumping me for Dina and Paris. It was all in the past and too petty anyway.

But Ashley was gazing around the room. "It's perfect," she said. "Like a cottage in a story. Why didn't you tell me?"

Suddenly I lived in this storybook cottage, and it was as good as her house next door to Los Alamitos Country Club, maybe better. Her eye fell on the quilt draped over the sofa back, the quilt Mom had been piecing all summer, getting her strength back and her sight.

"You make quilts?" she said, looking back at Mom. "Is there anything you can't do?" She didn't gush, only smiled privately for Mom. And Mom had come closer, and I wondered if she was drawn by the Ashley magic.

We sat down at the kitchen table to drink Pepsi Light.

104

When Mom started to drift away, Ashley said, "No. Stay." Because now we were above having to hide from our mothers. Junior year unfolded before me at that kitchen table, for us all.

Ashley has a way with adults. After a moment or two they forget she isn't one. She saw the scar on Mom's cheek and the other one in her eyebrow. She didn't flinch from them. "Will you be in charge of ISS again?"

Mom shook her head. "The school's decided to hire a man to cover ISS. I'm not sure if that's sound reasoning, but it's their idea of a solution. I'll be doing individual counseling, which is a step in the right direction."

Ashley nodded, following Mom's career. Mom didn't go on to say how she wanted Miss Wilmot's job next year, as college counselor. Maybe she supposed Ashley could see that for herself.

The three of us talked a long time, letting it roll. We even talked about boys in front of Mom, at least about Craig and Pod, and it was fine because we were so much older than they were, really.

I must have gotten carried away, because I said, "Actually, I'm not sure what Pod sees in me."

Mom sort of blinked at that, but Ashley said, "But you're his type."

"I'm not," I said. "We don't seem to see eye to eye on anything. Sometimes I think he's really looking for somebody completely different, or wants me to be completely different."

"I don't mean that," Ashley said. "I mean you're the type he's attracted to. After all, you're really great-looking."

105

I noticed she glanced at my hair, which I'd copied from her.

"I'm not. I hate my looks."

"So did I at your age," Mom said. She was probably just saying that to cheer me up. I think she's always been . . . confident. I'll never believe she was ever an adolescent.

"Every girl wonders what a boy sees in her," Mom said, "and every boy wonders what a girl sees in him."

"And what about adults?" Ashley said, though she never bothered much about grown-ups.

Mom just turned her hand over. "Oh, well, in lots of ways being an adult is easier. You come to terms with yourself. And you're far surer of who your friends are."

Timing her visit, Ashley was getting ready to go. Maybe Mom was timing herself too. "It was nice of Celia to call me after I got out of the hospital."

That was the first time I ever saw Ashley caught totally off guard. She almost sat down again. She glanced at me, but I hadn't known. Mom occasionally told me things I hadn't heard, but I'd have heard that.

"I wish I could get her involved in the parents' organization at Crestwood," Mom said.

It gave Ashley the moment she needed. "That would be marvelous," she said. "You two ought to know each other."

It knocked me out. Her dad's whatever—mistress—playing the parent role at school and Ashley approving? That was more than mature.

"See you at school," she said to me, and to Mom: "Thanks for everything, Mrs. Olinger. You're looking great."

"Come and see me, Ashley," Mom said, but maybe only I heard that.

Then Ashley was leaving, busy and committed. I stood at the door watching her turn the car neatly and start to zoom away. But she braked suddenly and called back to me, "Let's make junior year different." Then she was gone.

When I turned back, I didn't feel so open, not without Ashley there. I thought of swerving around Mom and heading up to my room, the old solution. But I guess I wanted to make it clear to Mom that Ashley was in charge again and it was right.

"She's pretty amazing," I said. "She's completely tolerant about Celia going to parents' meetings."

"Why shouldn't Celia go? She's Ashley's stepmother."

"Not really," I said. "Celia's not married to Dr. Packard."

"Yes, she is. They've been married five years."

"That can't be. Anyway, how do you know?"

"For one thing, Celia told me," Mom said. "For another, it's a matter of record. It's on Ashley's file at school."

"Then why would Ashley say they weren't married?"

"You tell me," Mom said, which I always hate.

"Because she didn't know. They're secretly married."

"Try again," Mom said, which I also hate.

I couldn't try again. Better leave it a mystery. Better not believe that since Ashley didn't want her father to be married, she just denied it. It was too self-involved.

Too childish. It was mean. Instead, I went back to that business about school files.

"I suppose you can just look up all kinds of personal stuff about my friends in their records."

"I can," Mom said, "though I don't abuse the privilege. I try to keep my professional life and my family life separate. I certainly did this past year, to humor you. I didn't like myself any better for knuckling under to you either. Particularly when we'd meet in the school halls and you'd look the other way."

Boy, does she bear grudges.

"But as Ashley says, we're going to make junior year different." Mom crossed her arms in front of her in a way I really didn't like.

"Don't start on Ashley again," I said. "I mean, she was here today, and look how nice she was."

"Very nice," Mom said. "She was mending her fences."

I didn't know what that was supposed to mean and didn't want to find out. "What did you mean when you said, 'Come and see me'? You said that just as Ashley was leaving."

"I don't suppose she'll come and see me—in my office," Mom said. "The ones who should rarely do."

"You make her sound like some kind of . . . psycho. Is that what you think?"

Mom waited awhile to answer, which I thought was insulting. "No," she said finally. "I think she's just a very ordinary girl who's had too much pampering from her family and everybody else. And she's quite a little manipulator. She's got a job for everybody but herself. That's why her grades are so poor. Grades are one

108

thing she'd have to take care of on her own. But she's troubled."

Ashley troubled? No. Gloria Raymond's troubled. All the Gloria Raymonds are troubled, but trouble couldn't touch Ashley. "Meaning?"

"Meaning Ashley wants the whole world to be the way she wants it to be," Mom said. "And the whole world isn't. That's trouble."

But I had to try for the last word. "I knew you didn't want her to be my friend. You've never wanted it."

"I think she could profit from friendship," Mom said, "but I doubt if she knows what friends are. Still, I guess you'll have to keep trying till . . ."

"Till what?"

"Till you grow out of it."

The next morning Pod came by for me, early. He was leaning on the horn before I was half dressed. Lucy, who was upstairs helping me get ready, went berserk.

Who's ever ready for the first day of school? It was even a pretty day, the kind you want off. Pod was looking good, which was also annoying. He's a somewhat better-looking kid than I give him credit for. Though he thinks L. L. Bean is a vegetable, he was dressed halfway civilized. At least his shirt had sleeves. He'd be great-looking if he'd let himself be. There he was, beaming out of his absurd car. It had the first coats of Rust-Oleum on it, looking like it had a skin disease.

"Crestwood, and step on it," I muttered, easing in beside him. This year I knew not to carry a notebook to Registration, so I had a hand free for the Danish I was

109

still eating. I happened to take another glance at Pod. In the lobe of his right ear was a silver loop earring.

"Pod, give me a break. Stop looking for these new images. On you they don't work."

Gazing thoughtfully at the visor, he reached up and jerked the earring off his ear. I flinched. But it was only a piece of bent baling wire. Anything for a laugh.

"Gal," he said, "you're lookin' medium grim this morning."

And why not? "Well, my mother thinks Ashley, my best friend in the world, is a manipulative brat and troubled. We're all looking at nine straight months of grueling school, and we aren't even seniors. And after slaving all summer at Sizzler, I've managed to save seventy-four dollars and change." I gave my Danish a savage bite.

Pod blinked.

"Apart from that," he said cautiously, "what do you like in the elective minors? I'm thinking journalism for one of mine and maybe marriage and the family for the other."

"Elective minors?" I rounded on him. "Who's thinking about elective minors? What about majors? This is junior year, man. Time's running out. We've got PSATs coming up. I've got to bite the bullet and take geometry. I've got to take French. We're staring American history in the face, and I'm still short a year of science. We're talking about chemistry."

Pod stroked his beardless chin. "Do tell," he said. "I'm getting around to science myself. They say if you join the Biology Club you get to go on a field trip and see a cadaver."

110

"Besides," I said, "we're going to make junior year different."

"How?"

I wasn't exactly sure about that. Then I had this inspiration and thought, Why not? I leaned over and gave him a light kiss on the ear, a quickie where the baling wire had been. I thought I'd just get it out of my system.

"Want to get married?" Pod said. "Engaged? Are you seeing anybody?"

Chapter Thirteen

Things were different, all right, including the high-and-mighty seniors—who were just last year's juniors, jumped up. They weren't so evolved, and being seniors seemed to go to their heads. We could see through them because we'd known them as earthlings.

And the new sophomores—where do these people come from? They were really pretty scuzzy, which was as big a word that year as *sleaze* had been the year before. This crop of sophomores were like puppies, always underfoot. They moved in clonish patterns you wouldn't believe. Let one tenth-grade girl start something, like tying her scarf to the strap of her purse, and every tenth-grade girl had to do it. Meaningless things.

"If anybody in this whole place is going to act like human beings, it'll have to be us," Ashley said. But actually the year belonged to Craig. He gave it a shape

113

even when we didn't see him doing it. It was the year of Craig and the C-Stars.

There was this club at Crestwood called C-Stars that was really traditional, going way back to the 1970s. We hadn't paid much attention to it before, I hadn't, because it was only for senior boys. In the early years a group of four seniors organized fund-raisers like pancake breakfasts and fishing rodeos. They painted curbs safety-yellow and worked with the Council on Aging. All the founders were planning to go into the Peace Corps or something. It started out mainly for community service and helping good causes and had a lot of status.

The membership was a big secret, but C-Stars were always the top four guys in the senior class. And what's better than a secret everybody knows? The community-service part of it faded somewhat, but the whole club was considered very important and subtle.

Every year in June C-Stars tapped four juniors as the new members for the following year. If we'd thought about it, we'd have known in September that Craig would naturally be tapped for C-Stars next spring, and with him Spence Whitfield, Gil Esterbrook, and Mark Gardner. But that wouldn't have been enough for Craig. He decided not to wait for spring. I guess that was inevitable too. Craig never waited.

It was outrageous, of course. No guy got to spend junior year in C-Stars. And typical of Craig's plans, they got going before anybody saw. We never noticed when he started working on the C-Star seniors, early in the year—making himself indispensable to them, lay-

114

ing his plans for being the only junior C-Star on record.

Then one day, history repeating, we got us another Gremlin. A bunch of people came to school and couldn't get their lockers open. Somebody had very neatly painted over the locks with black enamel. The little ridges on the combination dials were still there, but you couldn't see the numbers. It was chaos. People were spinning their locker dials like crazy and coming up with nothing. It didn't take long to notice that all these people were seniors.

"Hey, I'm innocent," Craig said all day long, walking down the halls, godlike, with his hands out, palms up. Ashley was walking beside him, laughing and not quite clinging. She was beside him more that fall, being where he was around school. But nobody thought he was the Gremlin. It was definitely sophomore stuff.

Then the Gremlin was caught almost before we could enjoy it. He was a sophomore named Blake Overstreet. He'd been this big hotshot in junior high, the same school Craig and Ashley and their people had gone to. And he was trying to make his mark. The whole Gremlin thing looked like a tradition in the making, except he was caught too soon. It was in the girls' restroom of the senior lounge early one morning before school. Blake Overstreet was caught applying a thick coat of Krazy Glue to the toilet seats. It could have been effective, because the glue was the same color as the seats and not particularly quick-drying. But he was caught in the act. Craig caught him.

But he didn't turn him in. That would have given Blake too much attention, so Craig let him go. Word

115

got around, but Craig only said he knew from experience that the Gremlin would hit the senior lounge sooner or later. Craig caught Blake pretty effortlessly, which was his style. Even a few seniors managed to thank him, and Craig got the attention Blake had hoped for.

⁂

Then one night at home, just a regular school night, the dogs wouldn't settle down. They howled and set up choruses and bayed at the moon except there was no moon. Dad couldn't quiet them and finally came back to the house for his shotgun, saying somebody must be around. Mom and I waited for most of an hour, but at least we didn't hear gunfire.

When he banged on the front door suddenly, loud, we both jumped out of our skins. Then when Mom began to open the door, Dad held it almost shut from the other side and said something through it to her. She turned to me and said, "Run upstairs and get a blanket."

I brought it back, and Dad reached around the door for it. After a moment he came in, and beside him was a boy wrapped in the blanket. Blake Overstreet.

It was the first chilly night in October, and I didn't know him at first. He was blue with cold and something else—fear. He was naked under the blanket, but he was wearing glasses. They'd left him that. His teeth were chattering, and he was holding the blanket around himself, tight.

I knew who he was because of the Gremlin business. So did Mom. "I'll make a hot drink. You sit down there on the sofa." She started to the kitchen in her billowing nightgown.

But Blake bit his lip. "I better not. I shouldn't have come into your house." His shoulders were bare and skinny. He looked down at himself, and there was a stain on the blanket, halfway down. I thought it was blood, but it was green. On the floor where he'd walked were spatterings of paint, green and gold.

Dad saw. He wouldn't have seen before in the dark. He ran his hand over his mouth. "Look, son," he said, "I'm going to pick you up and carry you upstairs to the bathtub. I think that's the best way."

He gathered up Blake in his arms and started for the stairs. There was this destroyed look in Blake's face. He wasn't a very big kid, not as big as he'd like to be.

It was oil-base paint, so it took a lot of remover and baby oil, and it had to have hurt. When Blake's parents got there, Dad was still upstairs trying to help Blake clean himself. They'd painted him between his legs, smeared a lot of paint over him there, in the school colors. He had some rope burns on his arms where they'd tied him to a tree on the lawn of the Pforzheimers' old house.

His parents were just these two worried people who wondered why their son hadn't come home from Cinema II. Coming down the stairs, Dad said, "That makes me about half sick," before he saw them there.

Blake's folks didn't know who we were or that Mom worked at school, until she said so. On the phone she'd told them to bring him some clothes, and they hadn't understood that either. Mrs. Overstreet wanted to go

117

right upstairs, but Blake's dad told her to wait down below.

After a long time Blake and his dad came down. He was dressed, looking like this kid at school again except it hurt him to walk, and he was pained and shamed.

His mother was really upset, and his dad said, "I'm for calling the police on this."

Mom looked at me and said to Mr. Overstreet, "There's the phone."

"No," Blake said. I could see he was this somewhat preppie kid, somewhat cocky. He was struggling back to being himself. "No police. Let's forget it."

"Forget it? How can we?" his mother said. "Do you know who did this to you?"

I knew then. I tried not to know, but I did.

". . . No," Blake said. "Just guys. They jumped me in the parking lot and brought me . . ." His voice wavered so he tapered off.

I could see he wasn't going to tell, so I thought: fine, that's the way to handle it. And the minute the Overstreets left, I went up to bed, avoiding Mom. After all, it was pretty late.

The next morning at the end of fourth period— Mademoiselle Hochberg's French class for me—the announcement came over the PA: *Craig Kettering report to Miss Larrimore's office.* Why did she have to send that message booming out over the PA? She could have sent him a note, for Pete's sake.

I didn't go to the cafeteria at noon; wouldn't because Ashley was bound to be there. It was a Thursday, chemistry-lab day, so I went to the lab early and sat there lunchless through the lunch hour.

I made it through to the end of the day without running into anybody by chance. The minute school was over I headed for the counseling wing.

Her new office was just a cubicle without a window. She was clearing off her desk and looked up, not too surprised, though I hadn't been there before. She had a new blotter and very orderly files. I was off my turf. For a moment she wasn't quite my mother.

"Mom, why did you call in Craig today?"

She raised her eyebrows. She was doing something efficient with her hair now, pretty severe. The ceiling light caught the scar, still white on her cheek. "Wait a minute. You spent all last year ignoring me, and this year you're going to monitor my job?"

I was standing there, trying to loom over her, clutching my books. She nodded at a chair, which meant I was supposed to sit down. She still wasn't quite my mother, but it was too late to retreat. I sat.

"I'm sure Craig isn't your job," I said. "He's not . . . assigned to you, or whatever."

"Then maybe he and I just had a chat," she said. "Do you think I should discuss that with another student?"

"No, just discuss it with me. You don't know that Craig had anything to do with . . . anything."

"With abducting and assaulting Blake Overstreet?"

"With anything," I said. "Anyway, it isn't abducting and assaulting if nobody swears out a complaint. It isn't anything."

"Isn't it?"

I shook my head, hanging tough.

"You oughtn't to be here," she said, "but I wouldn't have minded if you'd come on Blake's behalf. He's the

119

injured party, the victim. I was a victim, too, last spring, though I didn't swear out a complaint either.

"Blake is too scared and too immature to come to me for help. But we victims ought to stick together because there are so many people who couldn't care less. Like you."

"Me?" I practically came out of the chair. "How did I get into this?"

"By walking in that door," Mom said. "All the people who walk in that door are here for themselves. You're afraid I'll do something to damage your status with Craig and therefore Ashley."

She sat there a moment and almost didn't go on.

But then she said, "I know Craig was the C-Stars' ringleader in what they all did to Blake. Craig confessed to me. He liked confessing.

"He even listened when I lit into him. He liked hanging his head and looking suddenly sorry, but he wasn't. He even admitted that maybe he and the C-Stars had gone a little too far. It all worked out very well for Craig. He's in with the seniors, and he liked trying to con me. Then when he found he couldn't, he liked me better. He's only had praise from everybody else, and it's left him a little lonely.

"So you don't have a worry in the world, Chelsea." There was a touch of tiredness in her voice. "Craig's not going to hold our chat against you. Even when I told him I was going to keep my eye on him in the future, he was pleased. He likes attention."

Mom was reaching down in a drawer for her purse and the piles of things she carries around. It looked like this . . . interview was over. I guessed I'd gotten what

120

I came for, if Craig really wasn't going to be upset about this.

"Why don't you go on home, Chelsea? I'm not assigned to you, either, not at school. I'm irritated at myself for talking over another student with you. It wasn't professional. You got too much out of me, and you got it for the wrong reason."

So I got up to leave. What else could I do? I was dismissed, and I felt her eyes on my back till I could get out the door. It was eerie. She was my mom, and yet she was this other person too. While I walked down the empty halls, I got little flashes of Blake Overstreet, smeared and shamed. I got another flash of Mom keeping an eye on Craig. But I put them out of my mind. Anyway, I could count on Ashley. She could rise above everybody. For one last time I wished I was Ashley.

Chapter Fourteen

She never mentioned Craig's little run-in with Miss Larrimore to me. But Ashley had enough problems with him as soon as he began working on the C-Stars. From the first of the year she must have seen Craig slipping away. Finally she decided to do something about that.

"Absolutely no more girls-only parties," she said to the rest of us. "Honestly, what do we have left to say to each other we can't say anyway? If we're going to get together at all, it's got to be with guys. This is not a nunnery."

And so that was when the pairs paired off. We thought it was a pretty advanced thing to do, since most juniors still moved around in packs. Did we turn into couples because Ashley said so? Not exactly, but yes. Mark Gardner and Dina Westervelt. Landis Williamson and Spence Whitfield. Lauren Sperling and

Somebody Older. Meredith Hastings and Gil Ester-brook.

Me and Pod?

Everybody said it was inevitable anyway. Mark Gardner was already talking prelaw, so Dina of the very political Westervelts was right for him. Besides, he was short.

Landis and Spence were an obvious match. He was by far the top junior on the varsity tennis team, and she didn't even play, so they wouldn't be competitive. She's really beautiful, kind of bird-fragile and languid. Spence is more froglike, with a lot of nervous energy. I'm not sure why they were such an obvious match, but everybody said so.

Lauren Sperling reached out of the group for Rod Freeman, whose parents were friends of her parents. He should have been in his second year at State, but he'd dropped out a year to help in his family's business, or he'd flunked out, depending on who you talked to.

Picking somebody older was exactly right for Lauren. Her hair was jet-black, shaped helmetlike, no matter what style was in. She looked twenty at least. Rod was only three years older than the rest of us, so he wasn't exactly an adult, but it was more original than picking a senior. And he'd been to college, even if he wasn't there now. He always wore a Kappa Sig pin, but I didn't know how good a fraternity it was.

"In the middle," Ashley said. "Not great."

I don't know about Meredith and Gil. They may have been a couple because they were the only two left. And then there was me and Pod.

He worked for Dad now on Saturdays, which meant

they were under the Mercury most of the time. For a mechanically perfect car, it needed a lot of work. I walked up to it one sunny late-October morning and spoke to the larger pair of legs.

"Dad?" I waited till the sound of hidden wrenches stopped. "What would your reaction be if Pod Johnson took me out?"

Pod's legs were stretched out past the rear bumper below the tail pipe, still as death suddenly.

"Out where?" Dad asked distantly.

"Well, on Homecoming there's going to be a party. I don't mean the big dance in the gym. It's basically an orgy. But there's an alternative event being planned, a pretty select gathering, as a matter of fact."

"That right?" Dad said.

"Ashley and Craig are having a small do at Ashley's house. A sit-down dinner by the pool. You know, casual but candlelight."

At last Pod spoke, muffled under the muffler. "Yikes, the country-club crowd. Where'd I put that silk top-hat of mine? I had it at the opera. I know that."

Dad snorted.

"Of course there are plenty of other fish in the sea," I remarked.

"You can get 'em on the line," Pod said, "but they're liable to spit the hook."

"Or I could just stay home, which I'm not going to do. So what do you think, Dad—will it be all right if I go with Pod?"

There was silence except for maybe the splat of an oil drop on a forehead. "It's all right with me," Dad

125

said, "if Pod behaves himself. Otherwise I'll break his face."

"I think I can free up my social calendar for the evening in question," Pod said.

Which was all I needed to know, but of course they wouldn't quit.

"Say, Mr. Olinger, that's a mighty fine gal you got there."

"We like her, Pod."

"Another nice feature of her is, she isn't twins."

I went on back to the house.

Pod was a little more serious on Monday. I'd trained him not to sit in front of me, so he was sitting in the next row over with his big snake boots planted in the aisle between us.

"You didn't mean it about me going to that sit-down with candles, did you?"

"Why not?"

"Why not?" Ashley had said. "Of course you'll bring Pod. Look, if we wait for the guys to get their acts together, we'll be having hot flashes. It's time we got them thinking in the right direction. Otherwise, we'll be spending the next two years wondering where they are. We'll just be six couples having a quiet dinner on a night when there isn't anything else particularly interesting to do. We won't dress up, so tell Pod that. It's just getting together. It isn't *Love Connection*. And besides, you like Pod."

"For instance," he said across the aisle, "I don't have what you'd call a lot in common with those people, Chelsea."

126

"Pod, you don't know them well enough to know what you have in common with them."

"And that's another problem."

"Do you realize this conversation sounds like we're married?"

"You want to?" He leered lightly. "Are you seeing any—"

"Oh, shut up, Pod. And be there."

It was the perfect night for an Ashley party: summery in early November. We'd won the Homecoming game against Mesa Verde, and there was just enough breeze to flicker the candles in the tall hurricane shades. A long arrangement of yellow mums, football flowers, stretched down the center of the table, but there were place mats instead of a cloth. Because we were going to have barbecued ribs, we'd all be issued big bibs for napkins, so it didn't matter what anyone was wearing.

"Nice little spread you got here, Ashley," Pod said when we arrived. I watched him shaking hands with Rod Freeman. Then he murmured to me that Rod had a grip like a junkyard dog on a chuck roast. Up against my ear he added, "But he's wearing jewelry."

"It's a fraternity pin, Pod."

"Do tell," he said, but he settled down and acted pretty sensible.

We were all there except for Craig, so we mingled a long time. We drank cider from a keg and nibbled finger food. Craig not being there began to be the main feature of the evening, and Ashley was getting white around the lips. Celia—Mrs. Packard—moved in the

127

background, and so did Mabel. Finally she came out, her white uniform glowing in the dark, and murmured something to Ashley. So we had to sit down and start dinner.

It was supposed to be very grown-up. Ashley's parties always were, but it was a little too grown-up, with people talking across Craig's empty chair and wondering where he was and not asking.

He got there so late we were on the dessert. Celia had let him in and followed him through the house. Now she was hovering at the French door, and Craig was coming toward us, marching careful as a soldier around the pool to us.

"Oh, wow," he said, blurred from the first word. "Just go ahead and eat. Don't wait for me."

His face was bright red, beaded with sweat. His sleeves were pushed way up his famous arms, and he was swaying behind Ashley's chair. His jacket was stained, and he was drunk, really drunk.

Ashley started to point out the empty chair, but drew her hand back. She wanted him to sit down and she didn't. She wanted him to be sober, and he wasn't. He reached down and touched the back of her neck. It was all wrong, and she drew her shoulders up.

I had a vision of them then, mainly out of embarrassment, I suppose. I could see them years later, a middle-aged couple giving a party just like this one, and Craig coming home just like this. A fantasy, of course. Like part of another fantasy he reached in his pants pocket and pulled out a roll of money, a lot of it.

"While you p-p-parasites have been pigging out, I've been bringing home the bacon."

128

He held the money down in Ashley's face, grazing her cheek with it, and she looked away. He stuffed the money back in his pocket and spotted the empty chair between Meredith and Lauren. He went around and collapsed in it. It was Craig's almost unbelievably handsome face, but it was glazed over and the wrong color. You could smell him: liquor and something. Pod was sitting across from him, over the chrysanthemums.

"He's going to be sick," Pod said.

Spence and Rod jumped up and yanked Craig out of his chair. He pulled away, making a complete turn between them, and took a step in no particular direction. He was looking for the pool. When he found it, he went to the edge and threw up in it.

After a moment Celia came out, moving quickly, carrying a towel for Craig. He buried his face in it, then dropped it as Spence and Rod led him away.

The rest of us were still at the table. It'd only been moments. But Ashley pushed back her chair and walked over to where Celia was, still by the pool, retrieving the towel.

"You got here in a hurry," Ashley said. Her back was to us, but she spoke loud. "Were you spying on us?"

Celia's glance flickered over to our table before she said, "I saw . . . something was wrong with Craig, when he came in. I—"

"You don't miss much, do you?" Ashley said. I saw her back stiffen, and Celia's eyes. "You're everywhere I turn, Celia. I guess it gives you something to do while you're living off my father. I think we can do without you now. Go back to the house."

129

"Ashley," Celia said, "you're upset. I'll get your father."

"Leave him out of this," Ashley said. I never heard that much hate in a voice, welling up out of nowhere. "I said go back to the house."

And still Celia didn't move. She looked too shocked, and sad. Again out of nowhere, Ashley's hand lashed out. She slapped Celia across the face. The sound was so loud it echoed. You could feel it.

Afterward people said it was no big thing, that none of it really ought to count. Ashley'd just been upset about Craig. Actually, it wasn't like either one of them to act that way. People said let's just forget about it. But the party was over.

"Do you want to go straight home?" Pod asked me when we got in his car. I did. I'd had enough, more than enough. But I knew Pod was in no hurry once we got away from the Packards'. He could live in that car.

"I don't understand it," I said, meaning Craig. I wouldn't mention Ashley and what she'd done even though it was hanging over us. I only wanted to talk about Craig. "I know he drinks, but he can handle it better than that."

"You mean we didn't see what we saw?" Pod said. "I saw. I saw them both, in action."

"But Craig was like somebody else tonight. Maybe it's just something boys—guys—have to go through. Is it?"

Pod squinted ahead down the road. "It's different for Craig. I haven't been around many sit-down dinners to break up or many private swimming pools to barf in."

130

I stared out my window, but there was nothing but night out there. "You really don't like them, do you? Any of them."

He may have shrugged. "I had this feeling I was supposed to be lucky just being there. As a matter of fact, I've had better times."

"As a matter of fact, so have I—with them and without you. Has it dawned on you that you might be the snob?"

Maybe he shrugged again. "It's always possible, but if I'm a snob, I'm a natural one. You're working too hard at it. Did you happen to know you're a lot better person away from the bunch? You're more fun. You're more . . . real."

"No, I hadn't noticed. It doesn't happen to be true. You just want to turn around and take me home?"

He wheeled around at the next convenient driveway, pretty calm about it. The least he could be was mad. I was.

We were nearly home when I spoke, very mature. "Listen, Pod. Being a couple going out with other couples is probably a really bad idea. I mean, let's not force anything. We see enough of each other anyway. We probably know each other too well to go out."

We'd rolled to a stop in front of the house. "Have you got any idea what that last sentence meant?" he asked.

"Not specifically, but it sounded fine when I said it."

He sat there in the dark, possibly gazing at me. "Well, if this is our last date, how about a kiss? A real one—you know, all four lips?"

131

I sighed. "Pod, hasn't this evening proved anything to you? We've fought all the way home."

"This is my body talking."

"Oh, no. You're not . . . turned on by me, Pod. Don't play games. I'm not a voluptuous sexpot, even in the dark. I don't even have a figure, much. I have the figure of a praying mantis."

"Let us pray," said Pod.

"Promise you won't think about some other girl if we kiss, even if it is dark. Swear you won't think about somebody who looks like . . . Landis Williamson."

"Is this a court of law?" Pod said. "Am I under oath?"

"No."

"Then I swear it."

132

Chapter Fifteen

It could have been a great year, very social, pumped up. Everybody said so. Once the year got rolling, there was a kind of electricity in the air, even in the halls at school.

It was the year Camp Beverly Hills clothes hit hard, casual and classy. It was the year the guys wouldn't have minded looking like Emilio Estevez, and there were a lot of little Molly Ringwalds running around, in hats. It could have been a lot of fun, because there was partying in the air. It was Sheila E. in the background singing "The Glamorous Life," and a lot of Tina Turner, turned up.

Ashley's plan for pairing off seemed to work for everybody but her. I wasn't worried. I knew she'd come up with a plan. And all the other couples seemed to be hanging in there. Even me and Pod, I guess. I wasn't about to take him too seriously. After all, he was only a

133

junior. But we seemed to be turning into this uncommitted semicouple, whatever works. Maybe because of him, I began to notice more—to see school as a somewhat bigger place. The crowds in the halls weren't quite so faceless.

You had your Deadheads in their Jerry Garcia T-shirts and your goat-ropers riding the bus. It was the year for punked-out spiked hair that spread through several groups. Guys even: spiked on top, close on the sides. It was the year you noticed the Asian kids streaming out of the gifted classes, very starchy and intense, with calculators. And the Chicano kids pairing and pursuing, weaving patterns in hot colors.

Even some of the hard-core sweats were cleaning up their acts. A few of them were reaching for a Ralph Macchio look. One or two made it all the way to Tony Danza. It could have been a lot of reasonably mindless fun.

But then this mysterious figure came out of nowhere and started raining all over our parade, this so-called "Phillip Ogden Davies."

Like Craig, he started slow. He wrote for the school newspaper, just an occasional article. The paper's the Crestwood *Call,* and it's really pretty good. It wins national awards for high school journalism. People even read it. Every once in a while there'd be an article by "Phillip Ogden Davies." As it happened, there didn't seem to be anybody in school by that name, but it was right there as a byline in the paper.

One of the early articles was a small, savage satire about the smoking areas at school, the lounge the seniors smoke in, and the field across the road desig-

134

nated for everybody else. The article was this grim little comedy about how adults are really into their bodies now: jogging, dieting, going to gyms, and of course quitting cigarettes, while high-school students demand smoking privileges at school. The piece wound up with the smoking field across the road turned into a graveyard for a generation who'd wiped themselves out with lung disease. The last scene pictured bunches of very healthy, tanned parents in running gear jogging over to the field to leave flowers on their kids' graves.

It was pretty effective and got some attention. The city newspaper picked it up and reprinted it. A few Crestwood people actually wrote letters to the editor of the *Call* to say smoking is a personal decision, especially for people old enough to vote and fight, practically, and this is not a police state yet, et cetera.

Another Phillip Ogden Davies piece was more low-key, about a Department of Education study showing that American students ranked last among thirteen nations in math skills. Nobody was interested enough to write in about that, but it started a rumor that "Phillip Ogden Davies" was actually somebody on the faculty, in disguise. Because who else would bring up stuff like this?

"Whose newspaper is this, anyway?" people said. But then weeks would go by, and the mysterious grouch, Phillip Ogden Davies, seemed to lie low, or in wait. He struck again the week after Homecoming. The *Call* carried an article titled:

HOMECOMING MEMORIES:
THE GREEN AND GOLDEN YEARS

Another rousing Homecoming, that hoary tradition, is behind us, and a good time was probably had by all. Even scuzzy Mesa Verde helped when our Crusaders trounced their tails, and Shar Watson's Pep Squad yelled Crestwood glory to the November skies.

Here we hunker in heaps of green and gold crepe paper that turned the familiar gym into a pleasure palace rivaling some of your major discos. Who can forget the blasting musical offerings of that regional group-of-choice, Laughing Iguana, not to mention their light show, while the cream of Crestwood boogied across the floor from bankboard to bankboard. Who's going to mess with memories like these, especially if you're sober enough to remember them?

A special vote of thanks to that Secretest of Secret Societies, C-Stars, who provided the liquid refreshment at more-or-less reasonable cost and all going for a good cause probably.

Who's going to quibble over a night flowing with fairly good brands of the hard stuff, women, and song? Let's hear it for the C-Stars, that mostly senior organization of do-gooders. It'd be a dry old world without them.

But the problem is—even the gym parking lot is school property, though it looked a lot like an outdoor package store on Homecoming night. Probably if we dug around, we'd find some old

136

fascist law on the books against the sale of liquor
on school property. We might even find another
one outlawing the sale of liquor to minors, even
though we're all old enough to fight and vote,
practically. But are we going to let the long arm of
the law get in the way of a good time?

So here's to the C-Stars, those mysterious men,
Who can pep up an evening with vodka and gin,
And off to your parties all Crestwood will flock,
As long as you guys don't drink up your stock.

—PHILLIP OGDEN DAVIES

People really read that article. They stood around
the halls reading it, and they didn't like it. I guess I
believed what it said. If Craig and the C-Stars were
selling booze at the dance, it explained that wad of
money he'd had on Homecoming night, and the way
he'd been.

Though there was a tradition that no reference to
C-Stars was ever to appear in print, the article worked
for Craig. It was practically there in black and white
that he was a C-Star now, that they'd bent the rules for
him, and he was running their operation.

People thought that was great, but they didn't like
being told they couldn't buy liquor when and where
they wanted to. Craig was providing a pretty valuable
service. For a while practically everybody had carried
around fake ID. Then the liquor stores stopped ac-
cepting them, so a lot of people tried changing the
birth dates on their driver's licenses, if they had them.
That led to some trouble too. So nobody was in a

137

position to question how Craig's bunch got the liquor, in quantity. There's always a way. They were just glad he had it, and they weren't happy about him being hassled. Somebody broke out the windshield of Mrs. Fiore's car. She was the faculty advisor for the newspaper, but that might not have had anything to do with it.

It wasn't a particularly big deal, and anyway the holidays were coming. But there were . . . repercussions. In fact, that newspaper article led to a scene between Lauren Sperling and Shar Watson, of all people.

Lauren and Shar didn't even really live in the same world, but they had one thing in common. Shar was head of the Pep Squad, and Lauren was gunning for the presidency of Girls' Club. Even the clubs had nothing to do with each other, but they were both planning dances. The Pep Squad dance, cosponsored with the Athletic Association, was to be the big event of Shar's senior year. And the Girls' Club dance needed to be perfect if Lauren was to be sure of the presidency.

We all happened to have PE together, including Ashley. It was interpretive dance. Being on the Pep Squad, Shar didn't even have to take PE, but she was a real jock. Being a senior, she was also pretty overbearing.

One day we were all in the locker room when Lauren came banging in the door with her black eyes snapping. Shar was sitting on a bench, half into her leotard, when Lauren came up to her.

"Shar, what is this I hear about you moving the Pep Squad dance out of the gym?"

Shar wasn't even used to being spoken to by Lauren, or by anybody from Ashley's group. Shar had her own people, too, of course, not a classy bunch. Most of

138

them were her Pep Squaders with a couple of others less energetic, but seniors. None of them were in the locker room for her.

"We're having the dance at the Rod and Gun Club," Shar said, "if it's any of your business. The Athletic Association guys are all for it."

"They would be." Lauren's hands were on her hips. "What's wrong with the gym, as if I didn't know?"

"Since you're so brilliant," Shar said, "why ask?"

"Because I want to hear you say it, Shar." I'd never seen Lauren mad, but this made up for it.

Shar heaved a big sigh, which with her bust is a real production. "Ever since that piece in the paper, the C-Stars say they aren't going to sell booze at an event in the gym. It's just basically a business risk they aren't willing to take. The Rod and Gun Club's five miles out in the country, so there won't be any hassles. Who's going to turn out for a dance without anything to drink?"

Lauren just stood there, thinking about her own dance, the Christmas formal, which had to be in the gym. It was a charity thing, and they couldn't pay for a place to have it. We'd heard her plans before, in detail. Then she turned away from Shar, to Ashley, who was standing very still by her locker.

People were streaming out of the locker room. Shar went, too, gladly. And Lauren said to Ashley, "How are we ever going to have another dance in the gym? Who'll bother to come to mine?"

"It's all because of that dumb thing in the *Call*," Ashley said in a voice not nearly strong enough.

"No," Lauren said. "It's because of Craig. He's de-

139

ciding where we have dances. He's calling the shots. It wouldn't be so bad if he really needed the money. He's just in it for the power. There's something pretty sick about an ego that big."

Ashley's chin came up. "And you're not in Girls' Club for the power, Lauren? Then why are you so worried about that dance of yours? Besides, what am I supposed to do about it?"

Lauren gave her a long look. "I've backed you up a lot, Ashley. Now it's your turn. You see to it that Craig tells Shar and her crowd that he won't be selling liquor at the Rod and Gun Club. You know if her dance is a success, nobody'll ever use the gym again. Just tell him, Ashley."

The world turned upside down. Nobody'd ever challenged Ashley before. I was afraid to look at her face and couldn't help it. She looked scared. I guess we all three knew then. She was afraid of losing Craig, and she wasn't going to say a word to him. Lauren saw. She walked away from Ashley, and people don't.

Shar's Rod and Gun Club dance was a blast. Everybody said so. None of us went, but it drew the rowdy crowd, and they were never rowdier. "Phillip Ogden Davies" didn't write about it, but then he didn't have to. People talked about it for days, and the word was that Craig and his C-Stars had cleaned up. You could have bought about anything you wanted at Shar's dance.

So we really tried to get behind Lauren's Christmas dance, to make it work. I bought tickets for it with my own money, for me and Pod.

140

"Formal?" he said. "Sorry. Busy."

"No, Pod, you're not busy. You and I are going to the GC Christmas formal."

Pod pulled on his straggly chin. We were in American history, and he was gazing around like he wanted to change his seat. "Beg me a little."

"Pod, if we don't go to that dance, I'll make the rest of your year a living—"

"That's enough," he said. "Pick you up around nine?"

"Let's double," Ashley said at lunch one day. Lauren was busy all the time with ticket sales and arrangements, so that might have been why she wasn't sitting with the rest of us. "You know, double-date like people used to."

That was her way of saying that she and Craig would be going, maybe even that she had him back under control. Lauren wasn't sitting with her these days, even in Advisory. But Ashley did her best to help get the GC dance off the ground, selling tickets and talking it up.

She'd let Lauren down about Shar's dance, and now she was really trying to make up for it. I was gearing up for the dance myself. No matter what, this was going to be my first formal dance. Make that my first dance of any kind.

Then Pod said, "Double-date with Ashley and Craig? No, indeed. He wouldn't want to ride in my car, and I don't want to ride in his. We'll see them at the dance."

"But—"

"No buts. And I'm renting a tux."

That news stunned me into silence.

141

Chapter Sixteen

Nothing looked right. In black I looked like a corpse. In red I looked like Santa's elf. We settled for blue with cap sleeves and a tea-length skirt I could move in, and silver shoes.

I was coming down the stairs at home, touching the banister for balance, and luck. I was a home movie of Somebody's First Dance. Mom and Dad were down in the living room, standing close together, and in front of them Pod.

It's amazing what a tuxedo does for a man. They should wear them to school. It gave him shoulders, and arms. He seemed to be half a head taller. And he'd combed his hair. You could see the part. And something was in his hands: two camellias, rosy red with silver ribbon. Is this happening? Is this us? Mom and Dad were holding hands.

The suave new Pod looked up at my descending self

and spoke. "Chelsea, gal, you are my flavor of the month."

You take what you can get. Then, because life isn't quite a movie, Lucy shot down the stairs right between my feet in those teetering shoes, and I had to grab the banister with both hands to keep from riding her down.

The band wasn't bad, but a little muffled. The gym's acoustics aren't that great, and there was a lot of empty space to fill up. There were only forty couples, tops, and we danced a lot to look like more. Pod and I danced, nothing close or he walked all over me. But there was plenty of room. Even the decorations looked a little thin.

"They won't break even," Pod said. "They'll be in hock to pay the band."

All the Girls' Club members were there, but most of them on their own, without guys. Lauren and Rod were in a group with Meredith and Gil, Dina and Mark, Landis and Spence. But Lauren kept breaking away to circulate: checking the door where they were taking tickets, talking to the band, having the lights turned up, then down. In black she didn't look like a corpse. She looked like a tense adult trying to make a party go.

"At least everybody's sober," Landis said, but that was before Craig got there.

He and Ashley came late. She looked wonderful, in winter-white with the diamond earrings. Craig in a tux looked like he wore one every night. They made an entrance, and it was as close to a high moment as the evening had. Craig was there, and every eye was on him, and he let Ashley cling to his arm. People danced nearer them, drawn.

144

When they came toward the rest of us, Ashley floated a little—eager. But Lauren drifted away and took Rod with her. It should have worked for Ashley. She had Craig there, without his C-Stars. She was really trying.

But it didn't quite happen, because the dance wasn't happening. It was dead before it began, and Craig was the reason. This would be the last dance in the gym, and it was Lauren's. There was no way around that.

People wanted to leave early. I wouldn't have minded going. I wish we had. But everybody said, "Maybe we'll get a crowd in after midnight," so we stuck it out, though nobody came after eleven. Once when we were dancing, I saw Ashley standing against the bleachers in that beautiful dress, alone. It seemed strange.

The band packed up about twelve-thirty, and we were out in the parking lot where the cars were dotted around. Craig's 450 SL was parked next to Pod's Mercury. Ashley was standing there hugging herself in the cold. Craig was lounged against the back bumper of his car. It reminded me of the first time I ever saw him, leaning back against his stepfather's station wagon.

He'd jerked his tie loose, and it hung down against his snowy shirtfront. He was drinking Scotch out of a square bottle. All his gestures were loose and wavery. When he reached out for Ashley, she stepped farther back.

He saw us and said, "Hey, I thought this was a double date. Where you two been?" He ran his tux sleeve across his mouth. "Let's go get something to eat. Let's do something to make this evening live. Let's

145

go for pizza or something." The bottle slipped, and he grappled with it.

"Where?" Pod said. "Gino's? Lead the way."

Craig reached over and threw open the door for Ashley to get in. Then he walked, careful as a soldier, around to the driver's side.

We got in the Mercury, and next to us Craig slammed into reverse. They were out of the parking lot and down the street while Pod's keys were still in his hand.

"Why—"

"Because he's too dumb to sell it without drinking it."

"I mean why are we sitting here?"

"Because we're giving them a head start, and we aren't going where they're going."

But we caught up with them, almost. They were stopped for a light, and we were only a couple of cars behind. They tooled on too fast. They roared along Artesia Avenue, which goes practically past my house and the front of the old Pforzheimer property, the quick way out to Gino's.

Pod drove slow, letting them go, until they weren't even taillights. I couldn't think of anything to say, about the evening or anything.

We were coming to the turnoff up the little lane to my house. When we were still half a block away, Pod swerved over to the curb and hit the brakes. I didn't see anything, but he was out of the car. In the glare of our headlights I saw something in the gutter, a pile of something. I don't know what I thought it was.

Then I was out of the car, and he said, "Go back," and I wouldn't. He was crouched, half in the light. I

146

noticed his shoes for the first time. He hadn't rented shoes. They were just an old pair of penny loafers he'd dyed black to go with the tux. That was the last thing I noticed before I saw what was there in the gutter.

I only saw her paws, all four of them loosely gathered, in the light. I didn't see the rest of her, didn't need to. It was Lucy there in the dimness, and Pod's white hand on her.

She got out if you didn't watch her. We'd often hear her scratching at the door outside when we hadn't had time to miss her. She'd roamed down here to the street and . . . somebody had hit her, somebody driving too fast to stop.

Pod's hands were out to me, not to hold me back, just to hold. "She didn't . . ."

"What?"

"Suffer."

"Let me touch her," I said, and he stood back. I went over and bent down to put my hand on her. I could feel her ribs through her smooth coat. She was warm as life.

But I was too cold to think, and that helped. Then I was shaking with the cold. Pod helped me back in the car, scooping up my skirts and easing the door shut. He went back for Lucy.

I didn't like it—being put in the car, being taken care of. It was too girlish, or something. I didn't like myself. But when he carried her past the car, I looked away.

I felt it when he raised the trunk lid, but I couldn't tell when he eased her inside. I looked down at the dress I was wearing and the flowers that were gray in the dark.

He got back in and started the car, all in one gesture.

147

I wondered if he'd gotten . . . something on the sleeves of his tux. He drove the few yards to our lane and waited a long time with the turn signal on, for oncoming traffic to clear.

When we came in the house, Mom and Dad were watching an old movie. They saw something was wrong. It was all around us in the air. Then Dad and Pod went back outside together.

"What is it?" Mom was holding the top of her bathrobe close at the neck. "What's happened?"

"Lucy." My voice was going up and down, bouncing off the walls. "She ran in front of a car."

I saw how pale Mom went. The room wasn't blurry yet. She sat down suddenly on the sofa arm and looked aside.

"Oh, that will hurt him," she said. "Your dad loved that dog."

I went hot with a quick jolt of anger. What about me? But that was left over from being younger. Dad did love that dog. He was foolish about her and said so. Then out in the kennels the dogs, the other dogs, heard or knew and started to bay.

"Come here," Mom said. She was still looking away. I was keeping my usual distance.

"I'm all right," I said, trying to be.

"I'm not." Her eyes were full and spilling over, and then I couldn't see anything either. When I moved closer, I was ready for her to put her arms around me, but she didn't. She sat there, slumped, with her eyes melting down her face. It took me a moment to see she needed something from me. I reached out, awkward about it, and the flowers on my dress got mashed. But

148

it didn't matter. I couldn't remember how long it had been since I'd put my arms around her. I'd been smaller, and she'd seemed bigger.

We held each other, and the room was so empty the sound of our crying echoed in it. The whole house was empty without silly, sloppy-footed Lucy careening around or blocking up the stairway.

Later, I took off my flowers and floated them in a saucer. Not everybody at the dance had been given flowers. Ashley hadn't. I should have bought Pod a carnation to wear in his buttonhole. I wished I had.

"Your dad's burying her, you know," Mom said. "He's up in the timber digging a grave, and Pod's holding the light for him." She seemed to be able to see them, and so could I.

When they came back to the house, Pod didn't come in, so I went out and stood by his car with him. He put his hands on my shoulders and looked past me into the dark.

"I wish I hadn't said Gino's," he said. "Boy, do I wish it. Maybe they wouldn't have driven in this direction."

I hadn't thought of that, hadn't gotten to it.

"But we don't know it was Craig's car," Pod said. "It could have been somebody else, going flat out."

And that was true. You couldn't blame them because you couldn't be sure. And blaming them wouldn't work anyway, or bring Lucy back. I didn't say anything. I just buried Lucy deep enough in my mind so she'd be peaceful after her busy, running-around life.

Chapter Seventeen

Spring took its time about coming. We all survived PSATs, though I did better in verbal than math. And we got through first semester. I managed to nail the conjugations of *être* and *avoir* for Mademoiselle Hochberg and how to calculate molar ratios for chemistry, so I bagged B's for my hardest courses. In interpretive dance I was awarded an A for turning up nearly every time and keeping a tidy leotard.

Pod continued as a closet student, never seen studying. But he embarrassed himself by showing up on the honor role. That winter he quit working for Dad to get a real job at Western Auto to support his Mercury habit. Though he'd started shaving his whole face, you don't notice much with blonds.

He gave me a Valentine from one of your better drugstores. It was a grossly big red satin heart. On it he'd written, *You are my catch of the day.* Whether this was

151

a step up from *You're my flavor of the month* or whether we
were just holding our own, I couldn't say.

We were halfway through high school, and the winter
dragged, maybe because Ashley didn't have any parties.

"We were probably all too close anyway, don't you
think?" She and I were standing outside school one
afternoon, feeling a little warmth from the pale sun.
"What's the point if it gets to be a strain?" Ashley said.
"Meredith and Gil are breaking up anyway, and it's
tense just being around them. And look at Landis and
Spence. They're developing into a real relationship
and don't seem to need anybody. They're not even any
fun to be with. And Dina's going to take spring term in
Washington. After all, there are limits. We can all be
friends without being programmed."

Then Craig tooled up, and she turned and ran for his
car, throwing open the door and getting in before he
even had to honk.

She hadn't mentioned Lauren, but she'd lost her.
Lauren had managed to be elected GC president in
spite of the Christmas-formal fiasco. Then Rod Freeman went back to college for second semester, so
Lauren was high and dry there. But she never sat with
Ashley in advisory again, or with our dwindling group
at lunch. There wasn't a break exactly. She just went
her way. I guess that was the most mature thing any of
us had ever done, but I'm not sure how much I noticed
it.

The winter was draggy, and by the time Skip Day
came in March, we were ready for it. Whichever school
won the Crestwood–Mesa Verde game back in the fall

gets a Wednesday off at just the time of year you need
it. By a fluke Mesa Verde had won during our sophomore year, so this was a first for us.

I suppose in the old days Ashley would have had a
party around her pool that night, an alternative event
for her people. But that was back in some other world
now. There were big plans for evening events all over
town.

"Are we going?" I asked Pod, stifling a casual yawn.

But who can be cooler than Pod? "We might hit a few
of the high spots."

"Skip Day has a theme," I said, "but I guess dressing
up for it seems a little too high-school."

"We're *in* high school, remember?" Pod said. "Quit
doing your Ashley imitation." Which shut me up. "Besides, we've got us a prime source for costumes."

Though he didn't mention it again till the evening of
Skip Day, I got the idea Pod was all organized. The
theme was "The 1960s Revisited."

Even on this holiday he'd had to clock some time at
Western Auto, so he came by for me after work. When I
climbed in the car, there wasn't a costume in sight.

"Where are we going?"

"For a little ride."

I kept still as long as I could. We were out past the
last satellite dish in the last suburban yard, on a sec-
ondary road. Pod drove one-handed and absent-
minded to sop up the beauties of nature. At least that's
what he seemed to be doing. You never can tell how
serious his silences are. Pretty soon we weren't even
meeting any cars.

"Better enjoy this," he said. "Being on the road

153

tonight with two thousand crazed Crestwooders could prove prejudicial to your longevity."

"Pod, where do you get words like that?"

"Off those vocabulary lists you made last year in Mallory's class. One of us ought to get some use out of them."

"I see. And where are we going?"

"Out to the old home place to see my folks."

That caught me by surprise, which was probably the point. I didn't have a clear picture of Pod's family. I'm not sure how often I asked, or what he'd volunteered.

Once in a while, when it was time for him to go home, he'd say, "Well, I better get on my hoss. Them hogs won't slop theirselves." But that wasn't too informative. I guess I pictured a broken-down ranch with a yard full of spare parts. Maybe a little old lady in an apron on the slanting porch and a little old man coming back from an outhouse.

"And they've got costumes for us?"

"Even a car," Pod said, making a turn off the paving. We drove between two endless fencerows, wooden and blinding with fresh white paint. You don't get many fences like that out here. This is barbed-wire country.

We came to an artificial pond with ducks on it. Greening pasture ran from there with nothing to graze it. Where the fences ended was a circle of white gravel and a magnificent house. It was big panes of glass blazing with reflected sunset and long mahogany decks suspended over lawn. It went on forever.

"Pod, are your parents, like . . . the caretakers?"

He shook his head. "They have people for that."

Suddenly I felt very pale. "Pod, you're a rich kid. *A*

rich kid. I'll never trust another word you say for the rest of my life."

"It's probably the best way." He pulled up with a flourish.

A woman stood on the flagstone terrace, an ash-blonde in what appeared to be an ultrasuede jogging suit and Reeboks.

"Pod, couldn't we just go home?"

He swung the car door open. "Actually, I am home."

It was his mother, all right, though she didn't look old enough. She looked like a very lightly wrinkled young girl. And she turned out to be friendly: smiling, chattering, hugging Pod, looking me over. Then we were in the house. Echoing over its sound system were the last moments of a Jane Fonda workout tape. My head whirled.

Lauren could have held her dance in the Johnson living room. There was an enormous fireplace and a lot of big, bright pillows tossed around with casual care. Out one of the windows a hot tub bubbled. In the corner was a big loom.

". . . Do you weave?" I asked Pod's . . . mother.

"I used to. I made everything I wore." She smiled brightly down at her ultrasuede.

A man appeared out of another large opening in this free-form house. The space behind him was lined all around in books. These people had a room for everything. He looked like a big Pod, and you couldn't tell if his hair was blond or white. But the sweater was Ralph Lauren's, and the grin was familiar.

"This is my pop, the professor," Pod said.

155

Pod's . . . pop put out a big, soft hand. "Call me Glenn."

"A professor?" How did I know if I was being put on?

"At the Community College," said Glenn.

"In the Anti-American Studies Department," Pod added, grinning big.

"Now, Pod." Glenn shook his head. "Political Science."

They were actually a pretty nice pair of parents. They didn't look down their noses at me or give me a quiz. But I was so confused. We sat around in the big pillows, and the cat had my tongue.

I managed to say to Mr.—to Glenn, "Do you also farm all this land or raise cattle or—anything?"

His grin was Poddish, but more innocent. "Oh, no. We came here when Pod was a little shaver. We were pretty bummed out about corporate America and just wanted to raise our boy in a relatively nuclear-free zone, someplace where you could really move in the rhythms of the seasons and flow with an organic lifestyle."

I chanced a glance at Pod, but he was looking in some other direction. Mrs. Johnson was perched near me.

"Pod hasn't told us a thing about you, Chelsea. You know how he is."

Do I ever.

"What brought your family out here?"

"My mom's job. She's a guidance counselor at school."

Mrs. Johnson sighed. "Oh, that's too much. I think

it'd be fabulous working with young people. Kids are basically so honest, aren't they?"

Actually no, but what could I say? Now Pod was pulling me out of the pillows and away. We were heading through the house to find our costumes. Beyond the kitchen he opened a door and there they were, neatly laid out.

"Welcome to the 1960s. Around here they never ended." He pointed to louvered doors and still another room. "You can change in there."

My outfit dated from the early days of Mrs. Johnson, based on a vinyl miniskirt short enough to be outlawed.

"What do I wear under this little patchwork jacket thing?" I said through the louvers. "It doesn't meet in the middle."

"Love beads, what else?" Pod said back, and Mrs. Johnson had saved all hers—many strands. "Better hurry up. My folks are a little overstimulated by all this. They'll be in here in a minute to do the body-painting."

The next twenty minutes are a blur, but then Pod and I were outdoors in the glow of evening, walking hand in hand to a barn revised as a garage. Behind us his parents stood on the rear deck of the house, no doubt waving good-bye. At the last moment Mrs. Johnson had pressed into my hand a couple of pamphlets about nuclear winter.

It was just barely Pod there beside me. He was wearing parts of an army uniform with camouflage pants and a big ammunition belt defying gravity around his waist. Completely covering him were buttons with sayings:

157

FLOWER POWER
STUDENT STRIKE FOR PEACE
OFF THE PIGS
MAKE LOVE NOT WAR
CHE LIVES!

His . . . pop had painted longer sideburns down Pod's cheeks and tied a couple of beaded headbands around his forehead. He looked kind of like a Willie Nelson doll.

I'd had a quick glimpse of myself in a mirror. I had my share of buttons, too, and beads. Mrs. Johnson had painted a realistic rose on my cheek and a peace symbol on my forehead. I had on a straw sun-hat with more buttons on it, and granny glasses. The miniskirt was like trying to walk in a rubber band. Did people really live this way?

In the garage next to a new Volvo was a disreputable little Volkswagen beetle with a PRAY FOR PEACE bumper sticker and a lot of other statements written all over a faded paint job.

"Needs body work," Pod said, "but they can't part with it. Evidently they invaded Washington D. C. a lot in this baby."

When we got in it, I looked down and didn't seem to have on any skirt at all. The light faded as we drove back to town, and after all we looked better in the dark.

"Well, your folks were . . . really nice."

Pod nodded. "They're a couple of good kids."

"But why are you so . . . different from them?"

He had on a pair of granny glasses, too, peering

through them down the highway. "The position was open."

"No, Pod. That's no answer."

"I guess I just never took them too seriously. They never made any changes, or grew up."

And I'd noticed from the first moment that Pod seemed the oldest of the three. It was eerie, because boys don't mature that fast. Or was that only what Ashley thought?

"My mother didn't have to grow up," Pod said. "She came from a certain amount of money, and they're still living on it. She was a rich hippie, I guess you'd say, and married the graduate assistant who taught her poly sci class. Around 1969, I believe. Berkeley, of course."

"It must have been a weird time to be young in."

"Not too different from now, I guess," Pod said.

"Meaning?"

"There's still a lot of people around looking for leaders, trying not to grow up."

I didn't know how personally to take that, but the little VW just chugged along, and Pod said, "Actually I've got one thing in common with my folks. I have a small itch to reform the world, but I can generally keep it under control."

He drove on in what was probably a pretty serious silence.

The Skip Day evening activities were going on all over town. We passed up the Gym-o-rama at school: tumbling displays and track events, played mainly to an audience of parents, probably. But we went over to the Deer Creek Mall parking lot for a miniparade with floats. Lauren's GC had a float honoring the Beatles,

159

with four girls impersonating them, lip-synching "Lucy in the Sky with Diamonds" on top of a yellow submarine. It was the best, but there were a lot of good ones. They also had a parking-lot Woodstock with look-alike contests for Mick Jagger and Elvis. All the Deadheads were there in tie-dyed shirts and skirts, doing their Grateful Dead impressions.

It was all kind of fun mingling in the crowds, having people read your buttons, seeing people in all kinds of gear that probably wasn't even authentic. It was fun being there with Pod. It always is.

"I wonder if Ashley and Craig are here."

"I don't know about Ashley," Pod said, "but Craig'll be around here someplace."

When it began to get late, we decided to call it a day. We'd had enough of the mobs, and my body paint was starting to itch. When Pod brought me home, Mom wasn't there. She and Dad had been at school chaperoning the Gym-o-rama, and Dad had come home early because a kennelman is never really off duty. He was in the kitchen with his sleeves rolled up, mixing a batch of puppy mash in one of Mom's best stainless kettles.

We were there, bristling with buttons, clanking with beads, before he looked over his shoulder at us. When he turned around, his stirring paddle got away from him and sank in the mash.

For a second he wasn't there at all. Then he said, "Oh, boy. Look at you two." When he tried for a smile, it broke in the middle.

It was too quiet in this kitchen. When I looked down at my slick miniskirt, I thought I could feel the stuff

160

painted on me. There was something so wrong with that moment I couldn't begin to think.

"The Sixties Revisited," Dad said. "I forgot." He ran the back of his hand across his bristly chin, leaned back against the stove. "It's nothing but a big joke now. It never happened, right?"

Beside me, Pod moved—stiffened. Dad turned away and planted the heels of his hands on the stove, shutting out the sight of us. I still couldn't think, not with my dad turned away like that. That thing that would sometimes come over him was over us all. I wanted Mom here. I didn't know what I wanted. Pod knew before I did.

"Mr. Olinger, this is . . . dumb. We just want to get this paint off our faces. We want to get out of these clothes."

But Dad was swinging around toward us, nearly Dad again. The tattoo of the skull and the BTD letters showed when he folded his arms over his chest. Then he said, "You're just . . ."

"Kids," Pod said.

Dad shook his head. "You're just doing what people do. Time passes, and things change. Some people forget. Some don't even know."

"You were in Vietnam, Mr. Olinger," Pod said.

I guess I knew that. No, I didn't. Dad never said.

"Up at An Hoa attached to a Marine company most of the time, until I came home."

"Born to Die," Pod said, looking at the tattooed letters. He pulled off the granny glasses when he realized he still had them on.

"Nearly did," Dad said. "An AK burst took out ev-

161

erybody in the point squad but me. They're just names carved on that monument now. I wonder why I'm not one of them."

You're not one of them because you're my dad. I nearly said that, blurted it out. But he wasn't there just to be my father. He was this separate person with a history. He was still my dad, but now I knew him. And he'd been there all along. I'd always loved him because he was strong and gentle. I never wondered where that came from, or where he'd been. I'd always loved him because he was Dad. And maybe because he wasn't Mom.

He was looking at me, the hard kitchen light making his brows shaggy. "I was flown home from Tan Son Nhut. It's the airfield at Saigon. They flew me home on a 707, strapped to a stretcher, and there wasn't a mark on me except for a little nothing piece of shell casing in my kneecap. You know what that means, Chelsea?"

. . . Maybe. I saw him as this boy strapped down on a stretcher, without his friends.

"I was crazy," he said. "I was crazy in the VA hospital and maybe longer. I met your mom, and that made the difference. Believe me, I didn't have much to offer her."

We heard her car then, the old Dodge bouncing along up the ruts.

"No more war stories," Dad said. He put out his arm almost in the old way, and I climbed in, not quite in the old way. He had this other arm out, way out.

Pod hesitated a moment, but he took a couple of strides nearer, moving in his old cowboy lope. Then Dad had his arm around Pod's shoulder too.

Mom came in and saw us—two hippies and the crazy old Nam vet, hanging on to each other for dear life.

Chapter Eighteen

Craig wasn't in school the next day, not in person, but nobody talked about anything else. You couldn't even call them rumors. Everybody was sure. He'd been arrested—busted in the Deer Creek Mall parking lot around midnight for selling liquor in pint bottles and brown sacks. He was selling to minors. A lot of witnesses saw it happen, his customers in fact. The other C-Stars got away, four untouchable seniors, but the police nailed Craig.

Everybody said it was unfair, but I thought Craig must have made it happen. He'd like being the only one having his rights read to him and being booked, the center of things. He'd like to see his stepfather bailing him out.

Though he hadn't been locked up, he wasn't in school, and that worked for him too. It gave us all day to talk about him. Nobody remembered anything else about Skip Day.

I came home late that afternoon because of a meeting. The junior reps to the Student Alliance had been campaigning for a junior prom at the end of spring semester. But the seniors wanted it banned. They wanted their senior prom to be the only one. Finally there wasn't enough junior support to fight them. It was a pretty pointless meeting. When I got home, a big station wagon was pulled up in the yard.

Craig was in our living room, and so was his father—stepfather. Mr. Kettering stood up when I came in, but Craig only gave me a little wave from the easy chair by the fireplace, so it seemed Craig was in control.

But Mom was there, still in her school clothes. "I believe you know Chelsea," she said to Mr. Kettering, who smiled and nodded. But then he was back on the edge of the sofa at the opposite end from Mom. Craig never moved, so, yes, he was in control.

"It's good of you to see us, Miss Larrimore," his stepfather said. "Craig's mother wanted to be here, but she's a little upset so she asked me—"

"I'm Mrs. Olinger at home," Mom said.

I decided this wasn't my scene and started for the stairs, but she said, "No, Chelsea. You're home. Stay."

And I was pretty curious. There was only one other chair, and I took it, across the fireplace from Craig. He sat with his sleeves pushed up his arms. He almost threw one leg casually over the chair arm.

"I don't see that I can be of any help to you," Mom said to Mr. Kettering. "Officially, Craig's counselor is—"

164

"Craig wouldn't talk to anybody else. He has a very high opinion of you, Miss—Mrs. Olinger."

And yet Mr. Kettering was having to do all the talking. Mom's eyebrows rose, and so did Craig's, imitating her, not quite mocking.

"Craig had a little run-in with the police last night." Mom had been at school all day, so she'd have known that. Craig watched her, waiting for her to say so, but she didn't.

"It was mainly a misunderstanding," Mr. Kettering said, "nothing worth mentioning, though it's troubled his mother. The charge appears to be selling alcohol to minors. Of course Craig is only a minor himself."

Mr. Kettering cleared his throat. I couldn't tell how much he believed in what he was doing. He was a really handsome man. In a way Craig was like him, though I couldn't see Craig going this far for someone else.

"He'll have his day in court," Mr. Kettering said. "We've managed to delay it until the summer. There are mitigating circumstances. Craig was under the influence of a group of older boys, seniors. What are they called, C-Stars? I'd say we have a good chance of getting it off the books entirely. First offense."

Mom smiled slightly at that. So did Craig. "You seem to have the situation well under control." She spoke with the level line in her voice she used for work. "What is it you want from me? If it's understanding, I believe I do understand Craig a little." She looked over at him, but their faces didn't match this time.

"It's perhaps a little more than that," Mr. Kettering said quietly. "We don't know how records are kept at Craig's school. This incident had nothing to do with school, nor should it. But if it becomes a matter of record, it could be damaging to the boy's future."

"Admission to college after next year?" Mom said, and Mr. Kettering nodded, almost relieved.

I couldn't tell Craig's reaction to that. It didn't seem too likely that this kind of thing would get on his file at school. It sounded like the kind of thing parents worry about. Craig didn't look concerned, but he was listening. Maybe he just wanted to see how far Mom would let herself be used. Yes, that would have been it.

"It'd be a great relief to his mother, to us all, if you could . . ."

"Remove anything prejudicial from his files?" Mom said.

I knew then they were barking up the wrong counselor. They'd leave now if they knew what was good for them.

"And what is your responsibility in this, Mr. Kettering?"

He cleared his throat again. "Well, his mother and I are certainly going to do everything in our power to keep a tight rein—"

"What about his association with the C-Stars?" Mom said. "Those seniors who've influenced him? This is the first time Craig's been caught by the law, but he has a long history of selling liquor to minors, even selling it on school property. He has a long history of worrisome behavior."

Mr. Kettering started to turn to Craig, but didn't. "I know the boys have been raising money. His mother, and I, have been pleased to see him willing to earn

166

some spending money of his own. I don't admit that
he's had a long history of . . . anything illegal."

There were a lot of things Mr. Kettering didn't seem
willing to admit knowing about. I thought this was
Mom's moment to confront Craig. I thought it was
confession time for him, but she didn't even glance his
way. The tide had turned. Craig had been too far above
it all to speak. Now Mom was closing him out, as if he
weren't there, or too young to understand. She let a
dead silence linger before she spoke again. "Craig's
liquor sales are only one side of his problem. He has an
alcohol problem."

Craig stirred. "Whoa," he said, but only to himself.
It was too late for him to be in this conversation.

"Well, they all experiment," Mr. Kettering said,
looking down, turning the wedding ring on his finger.

"Not all of them," Mom said, "and Craig's past that.
I think he's been hoping somebody would care enough
to stop him. He's been looking for his limits and can't
find them.

"He needs specialized professional help with his
drinking. It's so obviously a cry for help that I believe
he'll respond very well. I don't think he needs any
more of the freedoms you've given him. He hasn't
known how to handle them."

Mr. Kettering could hardly take his eyes off his
hands. "I'm Craig's stepfather, I expect you know.
He's never . . . accepted me, or my authority." He
turned to Craig, but Craig was looking at the wall, at
nothing.

"And yet he has your name," Mom said.

"His own father died, and I adopted him when I married his mother. I was . . . glad to."

"How old was Craig at the time?" Mom seemed to know the answer to that.

"He was three years old," Mr. Kettering said.

That surprised me, a lot. Craig had a way of making you think Mr. Kettering had elbowed his way into their lives recently. I was really beginning to wonder what was real.

Mom was on her feet now, so Mr. Kettering stood up. After a moment so did Craig. "I won't keep you," Mr. Kettering said to her. "I shouldn't have come. I was way off base."

"You came because you were concerned," Mom said. "I can't do what you asked. But I can do something. I know who the C-Stars are. It's an open secret. Sandy Hurst, Mitch Taylor, Randy Menard, Nate Cuthbertson. I imagine you know their families." She was speaking only to his stepfather, but Craig was nearer than he realized, hovering almost.

"If Craig goes near them again, I'll contact their parents. We don't have much influence with parents at Crestwood. But these four senior boys have all been admitted to colleges. I can tell their parents that the school will contact those colleges about their sons' activities. College admissions for their children are sacred to parents, as you know, Mr. Kettering. If these boys and their families thought Craig posed a threat to them, they might be able to deal with him in ways you and I can't."

Mr. Kettering heard her out. I couldn't see what was

in his eyes. I was still in my chair across the room. "I'm sure we won't have any more problems, Mrs. Olinger."

Craig started to follow him out. Then he turned back, and I braced myself. But all he did was shrug a little and say, "Thanks, Miss Larrimore." He spoke in a neutral voice, but his face was flushed. I expect he needed a drink.

Even after we heard the station wagon pull away, she stood there looking at the door. She was winding down, but it took her some time. Even in the dimness the red glinted in her hair. She thought about turning on a lamp because it was evening.

"Did you follow that?" she said to me. "I wanted you to."

". . . Most of it. They—Mr. Kettering—tried to get you to do something . . . unprofessional."

She worked her shoulders. She was tired. "That part didn't matter. He was frightened and so is Craig's mother. But they aren't frightened enough, and not about the right things. It's easier not to be."

She turned to the stairs. I saw how tired she was and something about her work, how hard it was. Then she about ruined the moment by saying, "You're thinking about Ashley, aren't you?"

As a matter of fact, yes. "Who?"

"Don't worry about her. Ashley's the survivor."

She went on upstairs, pulling loose the bow at her neck. I wondered what she meant by that. But I was like Mr. Kettering. I didn't want to know too much.

169

Craig took it well. He even went out of his way at school to say hi to me. He was the hero of the Deer Creek Mall bust. Now he got word around that he was phasing out the C-Stars. The seniors were graduating anyway, and Craig was setting up a new club, going back for his own people as members: Spence and Gil and Mark.

They even came up with a uniform, which C-Stars never had. They all bought letter-type sweaters in green and gold and put the initials of their new club on them: VDC—Varsity Drinking Club. Within a day or so Craig was back where he'd been, and better than that. He was famous as the junior who'd shut down the most exclusive, traditional club at Crestwood. People thought it was great.

So I didn't worry about Ashley. Then she came looking for me one day after school. Warm spring air was blowing down the halls from the open doors. She came along, springy, with her books clasped in her manicured hands. Ashley in her aura. I was reaching down for something in my locker, awkward against her grace. She stopped a pace away.

"Do you think it'll help?" Her voice was soft and throaty. I didn't know what she meant.

"Do you think your mother practically calling Craig an alcoholic will do anybody any good? Do you think it's responsible to condemn him as a criminal even before his court date?"

I didn't know what to say. Her voice didn't match her words. "Look, Ashley, Craig needs—"

"I know what Craig needs," she said, her voice still lilting. I could almost think she wasn't mad. "He needs

170

a little space, a little time. I know. I was too much . . .
on his case last fall. We all make mistakes. I've eased
off. That's what your mother should have done."

"Ashley, I've got to meet Pod."

"Pod can wait."

I jammed my books in my locker and stood up to face
her. She was a silhouette against the light.

"Ashley, no matter what, I wish you wouldn't let my
mother get in the way of our friendship."

She put her head on one side. "You don't get it, do
you, Chelsea?" And still her voice was soft. We could
have been talking about anything, nothing. "When you
first came to Crestwood, I was nice to you. There was
no particular reason to include you, but I did, didn't
I?"

I stood there like a statue.

"You know I've always planned ahead. I knew one
day Craig was going to need some help. He didn't
know. I did. I knew your mother would be in a position
to help him if he needed it, when he needed it. I
thought we might be lucky and he wouldn't need anything till next year—help to get into college. But I
knew he'd need something, and I really thought we
could count on your mother."

"Then that's why you decided to be my friend. Just
because—"

"Of course not." She changed then, from night to
day. She came back to me. "But it got us started."

"And this is the . . . finish?"

She moved her head with that quick little toss.
"Don't be silly. If this was the end of our friendship, I'd
firebomb your locker or cut big round holes in your

171

leotard—something subtle." She grinned, and all I could feel was relief. She'd slapped me down. Now she was picking me up, dusting me off. It felt just like it was supposed to feel: wonderful.

"But you owe me," she said, brushing past me, bumping our hips. It was a funny little movement right out of Shar's Pep Squad, and it worked. She'd forgiven me and I was glad.

Halfway down the hall she turned and waved, knowing I'd still be watching. I waved back and then ran out of school because I was late for Pod.

"How's it going?" he said, gunning the Mercury. We hadn't seen each other since way back in history—American history, fifth period.

"Great," I said. "Fine. All I want is for the world to settle down and be itself. All I want is everybody to be happy and friends and all like that."

Pod nodded.

"Let's just get through to the end of the year without anything else happening."

Pod was still nodding. When he's humoring you, he likes you to know.

"Let's drop the whole topic about Craig's bust and C-Stars and—oh, good grief, what if 'Phillip Ogden Davies' climbs out of his hole and writes about this stuff in the *Call?*"

"He won't," Pod said, slipping into gear.

"Don't be too sure."

"I'm sure. I'm not even in journalism class this semester."

"What?"

"I'm Phillip Ogden Davies," Pod said. "P.O.D."

172

". . . I knew that."

"You lie," he said, "and you know you lie."

"You have three names even before you get to Johnson?"

Pod nodded again. He was wearing his spring hat. The Caterpillar tractor cap with the ventilator holes. "I named myself. Took it from my granddaddy, who hailed from up in Bend, Oregon, and made himself a fortune in wood pulp. He was a mean old codger. I loved him."

"You named yourself?"

"When I was six. I couldn't go to school with the name my folks gave me."

"What was it, Pod?"

He looked shifty and checked his gauges. "Sky Fidel Johnson," he muttered.

I didn't even laugh. I thought I better not. I just planned never to trust a word he says for the rest of my life.

But who could quibble with an afternoon like this with the water sprinklers making rainbows in every lawn we passed and the bright day winking off the Mercury's hand-polished hood? I thought it was a straight shot from there to the end of the year. I thought if we could just hold our breath, school would be out and summer here, the summer before senior year. I thought we just about had it made.

Senior Summer

Chapter Nineteen

The seniors were planning their prom, and like all proms it was to be exactly like last year's but better. They were having it in the Grand Ballroom of the Hyatt downtown, and the main point was to rent bedrooms and whole suites upstairs for the night. The real parties were to be upstairs, and practically everybody was going to spend the night at the hotel until the next day and check-out time. It was to be a really liberating experience for the seniors, and a blast.

But then they began to get bad news. Some of their parents sent out a form letter to all the other parents. A sample fell into the hands of the seniors and went up on the bulletin board at school:

AN OPEN LETTER TO PARENTS
OF THE GRADUATING CLASS

Dear fellow parents:

The senior prom, a Crestwood tradition, is

177

upon us, and we have high hopes of a splendid culminating activity to remain through the years a happy memory for students and their families alike.

We urge you to dissuade your senior student from engaging private rooms at the hotel on prom night. A senior prom should be a supervised activity. Prom night should be a wholesome experience, and the parents' opportunity to take part by dropping in on the dance to see their children dressed in their best and bidding their high-school years a festive good-bye. We urge you to cooperate by exercising your authority over your child.

Senior Parents for a Supervised Prom Night

Attached to this letter on the bulletin board was a checklist from the seniors themselves:

! SENIORS BEWARE !

The so-called "Senior Parents for a Supervised Prom Night" is a splinter group trying to destroy one more Crestwood tradition.

• If your parents haven't seen this letter, find and destroy it.

• Secure your own personal credit cards for payment of your hotel bill. If you plan to use your parents' credit card, get it now and keep it in a safe place.

• Tell your parents not to drop in on the prom. Chances are, you won't be in the ballroom anyway.

178

Senior guys should spend extra time with your date's family when you pick her up. Stop back past your own house on the way to the prom to show your family your date's dress if they want to see it. *Plan ahead.*

• If your parents ask if you rented a private room, be prepared to deny it.

If prom night is to continue as a Crestwood tradition, we've got to have enough solidarity to defend it.

Seniors for a Prom Worth Attending

Unfortunately for them, solidarity was just what they didn't have. Half the seniors hadn't been in school since April to read the bulletin board. They lost some time getting the word out, and lost some more being generally paranoid about parents. Then the school got into it, and things went seriously wrong for the seniors.

The faculty fell in with the Senior Parents for a Supervised Prom Night and decided to chaperon the whole hotel, even upstairs halls. When the seniors heard that parents and teachers were cooperating, they draped the ! SENIORS BEWARE ! announcement with black crepe paper. They seemed to be stuck with a wholesome school activity, and they knew it.

But it worked for Craig. Word got around that the juniors were reviving plans for their own party, even though a junior prom had been vetoed by the seniors. It wasn't going to be anything official. It was going to be better than that. It was also going to be on the seniors' prom night. At first it just sounded like a rumor to make the seniors even madder. Then it began to sound like an event a lot better organized than the prom.

Finals week was practically too hot to think, way too hot to think in French. It was too hot but sort of great, promising the real summer coming. People wore Jams shirts to exams: big overscaled numbers in laid-back, loudmouth Hawaiian prints. Girls wore baggy boxer-type shorts in the same splashy flower prints. If there was a school dress code, it was suspended. Anything more than a tank top and you felt smothered.

We were lunching at our table in the midst of this scene, having one last laugh at the sophomores. Let one sophomore girl tie the tails of her Jams shirt in a knot to give herself a bare middle, and every sophomore girl had to do it.

There were just four of us. Dina was in Washington, and Lauren wasn't there. But Landis and Meredith were, and Ashley, of course. I was there.

"I'm thinking about a party," Ashley said. It was the Ashley of old, and everybody looked up. "Well, why not? What are we supposed to do, sit around and watch the seniors freak out?"

Landis nodded in her dreamy, none-too-quick way. Meredith didn't say anything. She'd broken up with Gil, and now Randy Menard had asked her to the senior prom and she'd said yes. The prom was on her mind a lot, and her dress.

Ashley turned to me suddenly. "Is your mother go-

180

ing to chaperon the seniors down at the Hyatt Friday night?"

I almost flinched, and nodded.

"And your dad too?"

I nodded again, but she was nodding, too, approving. "Good for them," Ashley said. "The seniors think they're so adult. Why shouldn't they mix with real adults? It'll be a real learning experience for them."

She looked around at us, waiting for us to agree. I did, but Meredith, the only one of us going to the prom, looked sort of threatened. For some reason, that struck the rest of us as hilarious. We laughed our heads off.

It was great. The four of us were at this battered table in the cafeteria, but we were four . . . women having lunch somewhere else. Somewhere sort of ferny and far from finals, with waiters. We were these four sophisticated women having lunch, quiche maybe with just a glass of Perrier, something light. It was fun the way it used to be, and we laughed louder to make people look.

Thursday night after dinner Ashley came by my house. Her little blue Mustang was pulled up out front, and it was too nice an evening to stay indoors.

"Let's go for a walk," she said, though she never walked anywhere since she got her car. I knew she had an agenda. She was so businesslike I could almost see an invisible clipboard in her manicured hands. She hadn't dropped by my house for ages—months. She didn't do that, but it was fun and different. She glowed in the evening.

I didn't think there was anyplace to walk to, but she

181

started out across the grass. She remembered to stroll, and when we went past the pens, the dogs put their paws up on the wire to watch us, or maybe just her. She wandered only a little, and then we were on the path beside the grape arbor.

"Isn't there an old house around here somewhere?"

"The Pforzheimers' place."

"Yes." She moved ahead, finding the flat stones of the path, lifting a low limb for me. We came through the trees, and the house stood high at the other end of the side lawn. The last light played on the orangey tile roof, but the rest of the house was dark, with darker squares for the broken-out windows.

"It's perfect," Ashley said, to herself. Then, turning to me: "Like a gothic romance." She moved ahead through the weeds, and now it was like the cover on a romance book: mysterious house with glowing young girl moving across a twilight lawn.

When we came up the steps, Ashley walked on across the terrace to a pair of long glass doors. She put out her hand, and they both opened. Hadn't those doors always been boarded up? And how did she know they'd open to a touch? It was spooky, but miraculous.

"Let's see inside," she said, already there. She had a disposable lighter in her hand, though she doesn't smoke. It lit up the long room better than you'd think, throwing shadows on the faces carved across the fireplace.

"It's marvelous," she said, "even the floor." The tile floor looked freshly swept, though I couldn't be sure because the lighter flame went out. We stood in the dark, adjusting to it. "Good acoustics too."

182

"Of course, there could be a serial killer upstairs," I said, "waiting for a couple of female adolescents. Did I hear the stairs squeak?"

But I couldn't scare either of us. Ashley was too busy thinking, and I'd never thought this place was eerie. It was too safely tucked away. It would have been fun to be a kid here and keep it to myself. I couldn't think what you could do with it now.

"I know." Ashley snapped her fingers. "We can have a party here." I couldn't see her face.

"Who?"

"Oh, I don't know. The rooms are so big, and the terrace, and look at the lawn. It's vast. We could practically have the whole junior class."

I hardly heard that. It wasn't Ashley's style. Her group was always smaller than that, hand picked.

"You know what this would be great for? The junior party tomorrow night—better known as senior prom night."

Now I knew why we were here. I could see the invisible clipboard clearly, at least the bottom line. It was way past time for getting organized. Everything had been decided, and now I was supposed to know.

"What could we call it?" she said. "The Non-Prom? No, I know. Let's call it 'Senior Summer.' After all, we're going into the summer before our senior year. It'll drive this year's seniors insane if we take over the title before they're actually gone. I love it. We'll have a band and dancing and call it 'Senior Summer.'"

She was leading me out of the dark room, busy and committed.

"You're not serious, are you?" I said, out on the terrace.

Her eyebrows, almost invisible, rose on her face. She was astonished, as if we'd already settled this.

"This place is too perfect not to use. It's the only place. We won't be disturbing anybody. Nobody lives very close, and your parents will be chaperoning the seniors. Why not?"

"I don't think we could get . . . permission."

"Who from? There aren't any Pforzheimers around anymore." The corners of her mouth drooped in a mocking little way. "Oh, you mean your parents." Here I was, practically a senior, and worried about getting permission from my parents.

"First of all, they don't own the property, do they?" She'd started down the steps, but she stopped and waited for me to be there beside her. "And anyway, they don't have to know." She spoke quietly, as if they might be listening from the trees. "They'll be downtown at the Hyatt chaperoning till all hours because, believe me, the seniors are going to need it. We'll be in and out of here without . . . anybody needing to know. It doesn't have to be that big a deal. And it'll be the party everybody really remembers. In a way you'll be giving it. In a way this is your place."

As she walked away from me, the place was mine for a moment. I couldn't really imagine growing up in a house like this, but for a moment it was real, the way Ashley could make things real. I was the kind of girl who fitted this house: rich and remote.

"We can't," I said, but she didn't hear.

She was out in the grass, looking back at the house. I

turned to see what she saw: the string of Japanese lanterns over the terrace the way they'd be tomorrow night. I saw light coming from the house, candles because she likes them and the house has no electricity. I saw everybody arriving in the whites and colors of a summer evening, Senior Summer. I saw everything in her mind, just the way she meant it to be. And there'd be music.

On the walk back through the trees I had to think of a way to break the spell, but she was ahead of me the whole way. I walked her to her car. Even in the crisp way she pulled the door shut and clipped herself into the seat belt I knew everything was all arranged, the deal was clinched.

She was about to start the car, knowing I was still standing with my hand on the door.

"Ashley, we can't do this. It isn't even your plan."

She didn't deny that, but she wanted to.

"If you were planning a party, we'd have been hearing about it for weeks. And it wouldn't be a mob scene. You'd be having it at your house, with place cards."

"That kind of thing doesn't work anymore."

"It doesn't work for Craig," I said. "He wants to have a party here, doesn't he? A big one—his."

My hand was still on the top of the door, and she reached over to cover it with hers. She never did that. She never touched.

"That's the point, Chelsea. It'll *be* Craig's party if we don't get involved and make it like the times we used to have. He's been pretty low ever since that meeting he and his stepfather had with your mother. You can do something to make up for that now. Craig will mess up again unless we all work together. You owe this party to him, Chelsea. And besides, it'll set the tone for all next year. We've got senior year coming up, you know."

I really wanted to believe her. It was always easier that way. Why shouldn't we have something fun for the beginning of summer? Why not that perfect old house tucked up in the trees? Why couldn't we get all dressed up and dance the night away under the lanterns and moon? Why couldn't life be like that? Because it couldn't.

"It won't work, Ashley." I hated saying it. It sounded too grown-up or something. It let her down when she was desperate. It wiped out too much and didn't leave enough for the future. "I'd help if it would help," I said, which wasn't much.

"If you can't, you can't," she said finally. A night breeze came up in the trees. We listened to it while she let me wonder if she'd just drive off without another word ever.

"At least do me one small favor," she said. "Everybody's charged up for tomorrow night. A lot of plans are already made. But nobody knows where the party's to be, except for Craig and his guys, and me, of course. We'll get the word out that it's to be at the Pforzheimer place. Just don't say anything to your parents about it. With any luck your mother won't know. Tomorrow's the last day of finals, and we won't even circulate the word till after school." She nodded toward my house. "Just don't say anything about it. Promise."

"You mean you're going to go ahead and have it here anyway?" I still didn't believe. It wasn't sinking in.

"Not here. There." She looked toward the path to

186

the big house. "If you don't feel like being involved, at least don't spoil it, okay?"

I just nodded. She was letting me off easy.

"And don't look so serious," she said, though she couldn't really see my face. "Honestly, sometimes I think boys aren't worth the trouble they cause. Take you and Pod. You were lots more fun before you got so involved with him. And you're lots more involved with him than you admit."

Then the car purred away. She put up her hand and waved, knowing I'd be watching for it. When she was gone, I turned back to the house, with my lips sealed.

Chapter Twenty

Friday was the last day of finals and ninety-five degrees and chaos. Only people taking exams were in school, except for the seniors, who were there in full force. There wasn't a parking place for blocks around. They held an all-day meeting in the senior lounge, and it didn't do them a bit of good.

The band they thought they'd hired had canceled. It was a group called Julius Seizure and the Roman Candles. They'd already cut a demo and were pretty good. They'd pulled out at the last minute, and the seniors were faced with having to hire a DJ to play the Top 40. The Hyatt had offered them the combo that plays in the hotel cocktail lounge, and that really was the last straw. Senior rage spilled out of the lounge, and if you were taking an exam, you could hear every word.

Mom worked a full day and then some. Pod had an afternoon exam. I was finished at noon, and walked home in the blazing heat. For some reason I was avoiding Pod.

I worked in the kennels in the afternoon. Some of the dogs were taking the heat hard. Dad was back and forth to the vet, and I was hosing down the runs. I'd short-changed my kennel work ever since Lucy died. I didn't think the other dogs would remind me of her, but they did. I'd get very brisk and efficient with them, and still I'd remember her.

Since I'd sweated through everything I had on, I turned the hose on myself. My wet hair hung down in hanks, and my shoes were full of water. Then Ashley was standing in the door. Her car was outside, the dust still settling around it.

She didn't even notice my condition. "I just remembered," she said. "Your father's around all the time, isn't he?"

"He's at the vet now. He'll be back in a little while."

"That's what I mean." Worry lines appeared above her nose. "Then we can't use your lane."

"For what?"

"For delivery—refreshments, decorations, things like that. We've got to get set up. Isn't there another way in?"

"The front road to the big house comes up around the other side from Artesia Avenue. It's pretty over-grown, but you can get through."

"I know," she said, "but those big gates have an old rusty padlock on them. It'd take forever to saw through."

The keys to everything are on a board in the kennels, all labeled. The key she wanted was right there on the wall behind her, but she didn't notice. She didn't understand about this place. I almost gave her the key. I don't know why I didn't.

"I guess you'll have to saw the lock off."

It didn't annoy her. It was just one more item on her agenda. She nearly went about her business, but lingered a little, wrinkling her nose at the dog smells.

"Too bad about the seniors' band," she said. Her smile was so wicked I knew there was more to this.

"Don't make me guess," I said. "What?"

"We've got Julius Seizure for tonight. Craig hired them away from the seniors, and it cost a bundle. Is that outrageous? It's perfect." Then she couldn't linger another second. "If your dad hears us getting set up over there, tell him we're having a picnic or something, okay?" She looked at her watch instead of me. Then she was gone in a cloud of dust, a real one.

Mom and Dad were leaving early, to go downtown for dinner before they reported to the Hyatt. They were dressed up, but not formal. Dad had on the blue suit we hadn't seen since Easter. Mom had on her silk dress.

"You two look great," I said, and they preened a little. I'd changed out of my wet kennel clothes, but only into dry shorts and a shirt.

"Are you going out tonight?" Mom said. "Did the juniors come up with a plan?"

"I don't know."

"Is Pod coming over?"

191

I really didn't know that. "You know Pod. Casual till the last minute."

Then, as they were going out the door, Dad said, "If you're going to be around, look in on the pups. They won't need much."

So I could say, yes, sure I'd be around. I stood in the doorway looking . . . uninvolved, as they drove out. They nearly collided with Pod driving in.

He climbed out of the Mercury, wearing white jeans and a denim shirt, but very starchy. "The Pforzheimer place?" He nodded in that direction. "Are they crazy? I take it your folks don't know. Were you in on this?"

"Not really. Not exactly."

"You were or you weren't."

"All right, then, I wasn't," I said, snappish.

"Come on. Let's get out of here. Let's go for a burger or something. You want to wear that?"

No, I didn't want to wear that. I wanted to change into a skirt and other stuff because I wanted to stop by the party, Ashley's party, later—just drop in, no big deal.

After a quiet burger he took me to a movie, and paid. It was a Tom Cruise, and we held hands, and it was the dateist date we'd had, and yet it didn't feel like one. When we came out of Cinema II, it was only a little after ten.

"Now where?" Pod said. "A ride?"

"I told Dad I'd look in on the dogs." But we never quite made it. When we were still blocks from home, we saw the cars pulled off and parked along the shoulders of Artesia Avenue. The traffic was barely crawling. People were walking along in the ditches, crowds of them looking for the way into the Pforzheimer grounds.

The first seniors were arriving from their prom. They'd heard we had their band and we didn't have their chaperons. Girls in pale formals and guys in white dinner jackets and tailcoats were picking their way through the traffic. People were all over the street, darting across in front of headlights. When we came even with the lane leading up to my house, it was completely blocked with more parked cars.

"I give this another half hour," Pod said, "forty-five minutes, tops."

"And then what?"

"For one thing, the cops will be here. What did they tell you, Chelsea? That they were just going to have a quiet little get-together someplace where nobody'd notice? And you bought it."

"I didn't buy anything. It was just that Ashley wanted to . . . get in on a party Craig already organized. She was just trying to keep him in line, and she was really worried. I told her it wouldn't work."

"I don't think she heard you." He had to gear down to first, not his usual smooth shifting. There wasn't a place to park for blocks. When he could pull off, we were facing out to a dark open field they were grading for new houses.

He just sat there. "What's the plan?"

I thought he might have one. I was dazed by all those cars and people, and I couldn't see a minute ahead.

"They had to pick this place of all places," he said, "right on your own turf, practically on top of your house."

193

"What are you saying, that Ashley and Craig were out to get me—set me up?"

He thought about that. "No. You didn't figure in their plans. You aren't that important to them."

I got out of the car and started walking back along the parked cars. I didn't care if he came with me or not, but he did.

They'd managed to get the big iron gates open, and you could begin to hear the band. The road leading up through the underbrush to the front of the house was too narrow for parking. But it was full of people moving toward the music. In front of the house Craig's 450 SL was pulled up by the steps.

There weren't any Japanese lanterns. But all the terraces were strung with colored lights run from a portable generator, and more lights inside, glaring. They'd pried the front doors open. And all around the house was this sea of people, and more pouring out from inside, carrying drinks, lining bottles along the railings where the old urns had been.

"We don't get this kind of attendance at school," Pod said. "Seen enough?"

"I've got to find Ashley." I wasn't sure why.

Randy Menard and Meredith were sitting on the front steps, deep in conversation, with people stepping over them. I saw her dress—beautiful and strapless. We moved on into the house against the flow of people. The music seemed to come from everywhere. A long staircase curved up out of the hall with people sitting on it, talking, smoking, drinking, all the way up into the darkness.

In the long room with the tiled floor the band was at

194

the far end. People were dancing down there, only a few, because it was still early. All along one side, flood-lit, was the bar. The bartenders were the Varsity Drink-ing Club: Mark and Gil and Spence, and Craig. They wore white sweatpants and had their shirts off, just bandanas around their necks. They had a big tub of ice for the beer and were selling the hard stuff in pint bottles.

Craig was taking the money, folding it around his fingers. Craig was there fully floodlit, dispensing the drinks, charging for them, making all this happen. The grin on his face matched the lights, and he moved in a rhythm that made his arms glisten.

There was a crowd of people around him, and he toasted them, matching them drink for drink from a bottle he kept pulling out from the drawstring of his sweatpants. It was Craig's night. He had the seniors' music and half the seniors themselves. When he asked them how they liked their band, they clapped and cheered. Because this was the place to be.

I saw Landis dancing dreamily by herself because Spence was tending bar, but I didn't think I'd find Ashley. The rest of the room was too dark and confus-ing. But then I saw her standing by the doors we'd come through last night when this was a deserted old house. The people moving right past her didn't seem to notice her there.

When she saw me, her eyes shifted to look over my shoulder. She smiled and nodded to somebody behind me. But it was too late for that. I knew there wasn't anybody there smiling and nodding back.

195

"Isn't it marvelous?" she said, her eyes still trying for distance. "I told you this was the perfect place."

"Ashley, let's get everybody out of here before the police come, or my parents. Let's get this stopped."

She pulled back, but she knew I'd follow her.

"But it's working." She tossed her head a little because this evening was working, and we ought to flow with it. "Everybody's having a great time."

"You're not, Ashley."

She pretended not to hear because of the music, and I was reaching for every word, hoping for the right one.

"Get the band stopped. They've been paid. Kill the lights or something. Be in charge, Ashley, the way you used to be."

She heard that. She winced and tried to turn it into a wink. Turning away from me, she looked across the room at Craig. He was handing bottles over people's heads, laughing big, bathed in sweat and laughter. He was out of her reach, and I guess I'd made her know that.

She turned back and smiled at me. "Run on home, Chelsea. And if your parents ask, tell them you don't have anything to do with this. Tell them you never really belonged."

A moan went up, not mine. It was everybody around the bar groaning because the liquor had run out. But Craig was in command, going for a fresh supply. He was going himself because he was the source of everything.

I caught up with him in the front hall. People were wanting to stop him and talk about this great party. But he was shouldering past them, face flushed, with the same grin for everybody. I took his arm, and he saw me, more or less.

"Craig, where do you get your—supplies?"

"From the steward at the country club, whatever I want. Everybody profits. I'll be back in a couple of minutes." His voice was only a little slurred. "You taking up serious drinking, Chelsea?"

We were outside, starting down the steps to his car, and I still had him by the arm.

"Just keep going," I said to him. "Don't come back. There'll be police cars here pretty soon. You know that. The traffic's a mess—and the noise. People have called by now to complain. Just keep going, Craig, and let's get this evening stopped. You've been arrested once, and you haven't even had your court date yet. You don't need this."

I knew then what my mother did for a living. She told people things they didn't have to hear.

The keys were in his car. He never worried. He stumbled but settled into the leather seat of the 450 SL. Just before the motor gunned, he said, "Chelsea, those rules don't apply to me. Rules don't."

He peeled away, made a half circle that caused the crowds to scatter back. His headlights swooped, finding the narrow tunnel through the trees down to Artesia Avenue. He kept flashing the lights to clear the crowds and touched the brakes just once, turning the tunnel of trees red. The car thundered out of sight.

Pod was on the step above me. He put his hand on my shoulder, and then we heard the sudden explosion of sound, over the music. Then the steady blare of a car horn. People were running, and the car horn, stuck, wouldn't stop. Pod's hand closed on my shoulder, tight.

⚘

Mom and Dad had left the prom early. There weren't enough seniors to chaperon, and she'd heard where they were going.

Because of the cars they couldn't get up our lane. They heard the horn that wouldn't stop. Then they came to the front gates Craig had been too drunk to drive through. One gate was hanging from a hinge, half collapsed out onto Artesia Avenue. The grille of Craig's car was folded around the base of the high gatepost. One of the headlights was still on, throwing a beam up into the trees.

By then Pod and I had run down the dark lane, full of people turning, running with us. The only thing you could see was this headlight turning the tree limbs a blinding white, and the taillights still red because of the jammed brakes.

Pod pushed through everybody, getting up to the door, trying to pry it open. Then Dad was there, elbowing Pod away, jerking the door open on Craig's side while Pod pulled the wire under the crumpled hood to stop the horn. Pod and Dad were both there keeping everybody back till the paramedics got there.

For days afterward people said Craig was dead. They'd seen him dead in the car; nobody could survive it. They described the star his head had made in the windshield and the steering column as a lethal weapon. They described in living color how Craig had died. But he may live a long time, in some gray world.

198

"You knew," Mom said later that night, lots later.

"Ashley wanted a party to . . ." The words went dead in my mouth. They were in some foreign language, and we'd crossed the border.

"You should have walked away from them sooner," she said. "Now it'll be harder. Now you'll be haunted."

Chapter Twenty-one

The Ketterings came the next morning early, from the hospital. We stood outside with them beside their station wagon. They hadn't slept, and neither had we, the five of us, without Craig. His folks came to say that he'd be brain-damaged and paralyzed. They looked for other words, but it came down to those. I wondered if they noticed it was Mom they turned to first.

"What you said about Craig made more sense than . . . anything else," Mr. Kettering told her. "But it was too late, you see. We thought we were just like other families. We were. When we couldn't control him, we just hoped for the best."

He looked away. His face was drawn, and he needed a shave, the way nobody ever saw him. "He was a beautiful kid."

Mrs. Kettering covered her face with her hand. She was wearing the dress she'd worn at a party last night.

A little morning breeze stirred her skirt, but she stood ramrod straight. When she took her hand away, I noticed again how much Craig looked like her. She wouldn't cry for her beautiful kid before strangers.

"We're grateful to you," Mr. Kettering said, "for . . . everything."

"What did I do?" Mom said. "Nothing. I'm supposed to make a difference for these kids, but I can only nibble around the edges of their lives in a job nobody really wants me to do."

Mrs. Kettering's eyes were wet and full as she gazed at Mom. But I guess she hadn't really heard. "Why did this happen to us?" I don't know who she was asking. She glanced around and didn't like this morning looking so normal and everyday. "It's all worse than if my boy was dead," she said, realizing. "Will I wish he was? This is the worst thing that could happen."

But Mom was shaking her head, running a hand up her arm like she was chilled. "No, not quite. Craig was in a car, drunk. It would have been worse if he'd hurt someone else, someone innocent. A child darting out in the street. A man going off to work a night shift somewhere. We let him become a lethal weapon. At least he didn't hit anyone." She looked away at the treetops. "That would have been worse."

Mr. Kettering put up his arm, almost to shield his wife.

"What?" Mrs. Kettering asked him. "What did she say?"

But he was turning her, and they were going. He put her in the car and they drove away. We turned back to the house, Mom and Dad and I.

202

But inside, she moved away from us.

"You heard what I said to them. It was . . . unforgivable. They couldn't do anything with their son. I haven't got any better relationship with you, Chelsea."

She stood, dry eyed, looking at me.

"I've been too much like any other parent, and you've been too much like any other child. We give you all this space and time, and you do nothing with it but damage.

"I should have known about that party last night. You should have told me. We should have worked together—two human beings. It was our moment, and we missed it."

I couldn't listen. It was too final, and too real. But she wasn't through.

"I'm quitting my job at Crestwood."

I looked at Dad, but I think he already knew.

"Don't worry," she said to me, wearily. "You can finish here, have your senior year. I'll find something else to do."

But she was talking to me like a child, like I cared where I spent senior year. "Go on." She nodded to the stairs, my old escape route. "We're all too tired."

I sat up on the bed with my old Walkman coiled next to me and all my stuff littered around. But there was nothing particularly familiar about any of it. Even the room belonged to somebody younger. I looked back over two years, and nothing mattered but last night and this morning.

When I heard Pod talking to Dad downstairs, I knew where I needed to be. Pod had stopped by on his way to work. I was down the stairs, long legs leaping. I got him out in his car before he could think.

"Take me over to the Packards'."

He was going to give me an argument, and I looked at him, and he didn't. When we were in sight of Los Alamitos Country Club and Ashley's house, I said, "Just leave me here. Go on to work. I'll see you later."

I leaned on the bell, and Ashley opened the door. She was dressed, and pale. The summer hadn't found us. Her gray eyes were red and swollen, but I couldn't be bothered with that now.

"Where's Celia?"

Ashley, surprised, stepped back, so I was in the front hall.

But Celia was right there, farther back. She was dressed, too, and I was glad of that. Celia's tall. So am I. I spoke over Ashley's head. "Come home with me and talk to my mother," I said. "I know you don't know her, but just come."

Celia didn't have her makeup on, so she looked older than usual. She hesitated, but we went out to her car, the Audi she shops in. Ashley was with us, watching me every step of the way.

But I said, "Not you, just Celia."

I banged the door of the Audi, and Celia drove us away. I got her to my house without saying much. Then we were getting out of the car, and I wasn't sure about this. But Celia was being nice to me. She's too nice, if you ask me.

Dad was out in the kennels, and when we got in the house, Mom had no idea who this woman was. "This is

Mrs. Packard, Mom. You talked to her on the phone once a long time ago. "Celia, this is my mother."

Celia holds back. She's that way. She lingers in doorways and isn't aggressive. But she said to Mom that they should have met before, since Ashley and I are such good friends. It wasn't the beginning I was looking for, but it was a beginning.

Mom was dividing her looks between Celia and me. Then she was pouring out some coffee, and we were sitting around the kitchen table. I almost regressed. I almost turned into this little girl whose mother is having company. But that couldn't be. We had to be three women. I had to be one of these women, and all I'd ever done was knuckle under to a girl named Ashley.

"Celia, my mom says she's going to quit her job at school. This next year she's in line for a promotion and tenure. She's going to throw it all away."

Mom shot me a glance. "Chelsea—"

"Oh, but why?" Celia said. She has a breathy, small voice for a woman that tall.

"She's discouraged—about Craig, about all of us . . . me." I took a breath and kept going. "People need her at that school. She could even help Ashley, and Ashley could use it."

Celia's cup was halfway to her lips, going nowhere.

"Ashley's had you right where she wants you, Celia. You were another one who saw Craig was drunk all the time and . . . hungry for limits nobody gave him. You let him into your house drunk, Celia. You let anything happen that Ashley wants."

"Enough, Chelsea," Mom said.

It wasn't working. I didn't know how to do this. I'd

slipped back to being a child blaming a grown-up, when—

"She's not wrong," Celia said. "I never have figured out what my rights are. Ashley's in the driver's seat, and I take it. I'm so busy trying not to be the wicked stepmother that I'm just barely there. She uses that. I suppose it wouldn't be any different if I were her own mother. I'm glad I'm not."

She stopped and bit her lip. Putting down her cup, she drew back into herself and stood up. They said a few things, smooth-over things, on the way to the door. "It's a bad time," they said, "for everybody."

But as she was leaving, she said to Mom, "I wish you'd stay on the job. People like me need to know you're there."

But Mom only smiled, being nice. When Celia was gone, she closed the front door and leaned back against it.

"It doesn't work that way," she said. "You can't fix everything in a day. Some things can't ever be fixed. You can't grow up in one morning, and you haven't been getting ready. You've lost a lot of time."

"But you won't quit, will you? You won't quit because of—"

"I'll quit my job. I won't quit being your mother. Come here. Stop looking for people to put between us. Come here and let me hold you. Hold me."

We were there for each other like the night Lucy died. Except that was an end, and this was a beginning.

And now it's August, though it took its time coming. Mom resigned, and she's working up her resume to show to the headhunters who'll find her another job.

None of us can see Craig, and that just fans the rumors. They say he's hooked up on machines that breathe for him, that he weighs ninety pounds now, that somebody ought to pull the plug. But nobody really knows.

He won't be there senior year. He won't be anywhere, really. But I dreamed about him once this summer. It wasn't even much of a dream. I just saw Craig in his sweatpants, running. It was over a field somewhere, no place real. He was just running, moving like a beautiful animal. His face wasn't even flushed. And there weren't any fences or anything to limit him. But now it's okay because in the dream he isn't looking for limits.

I saw Ashley last night at Deer Creek Mall, for the first time all summer. I have my old job back at Sizzler because I couldn't find anything that paid any better. They put me on the salad bar again. I've gotten a little miserly with my wages, so I saved up for some school things and went out to the mall. Ashley was coming out of a store, loaded down with packages.

"Oh, Chelsea, hi." She started to look past me. "I'm rushed off my feet," she said, but when she saw I wouldn't stop her, she lingered. "I'm going away to school this fall," she said, "boarding school back East. Maybe you've heard."

I hadn't.

"Honestly, another year at Crestwood? I just

couldn't, and told Daddy. Skip Day? Junior Board fashion show? The same old faces?"

Except for Craig's, but she didn't mention him. She was looking ahead, the way she does.

"I cannot *wait* to get out of here," Ashley said. "For one thing, Celia's getting impossible." She jiggled her shopping bags around to look at her watch. "And I'm late. See you." Then she hurried away, busy and committed.

In a way—not the old way—I didn't want her to go. I wanted to call her back so we could end our friendship. But there was nothing to end. I just kept walking. There was nothing to it. And I didn't look back in case she waved.

It was almost closing time anyway. Pod had done all his back-to-school shopping in about two minutes. Then he'd loped back to the Mercury to wait for me. He could live in that car.

About the author

One of the most popular and highly acclaimed authors of young adult fiction, Richard Peck is devoted to writing books for teenagers that will convince them to act independently of their peers. As he has said, "Books at their most worthwhile are the success stories of people who manage to prevail in trying times. No civilization lasts. But there are always survivors. And the survivors are those who have taken independent action. Reading a book is an independent act."

Richard Peck attended Exeter University in England and holds degrees from DePauw University and Southern Illinois University. His novels for young adults include *Secrets of the Shopping Mall, Close Enough to Touch,* and *Remembering the Good Times,* which was an ALA Notable Book and a Best Book for Young Adults. Three of Mr. Peck's novels have been filmed for television. His most recent book for Delacorte Press was *Blossom Culp and the Sleep of Death,* also an ALA Notable Book.

Richard Peck lives in New York City.

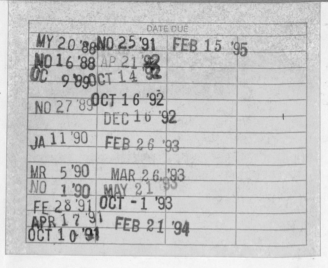

FIC
PEC

Peck, Richard.

Princess Ashley.